ACCUSED!

Dan got back to his cottage, the one-time gamekeeper's cottage under the dripping edge of the Priory Woods, when the sky was growing pale and the birds were getting busy. He was tired. But it was a merit of his way of life that, if he chose, he could spend all morning in bed.

Not that morning. He was woken by his mother, after what seemed like one minute. With her was a policeman in uniform, strange to Dan. He was to come along. He was to give an account of his movements the previous night. He had immediate and sickening visions of having been seen taking the horse.

The reality was even more sickening. Mrs Gwyneth Addison, neighbour of old Lady Dodds-Freeman, had been found by PC Gundry at nine o'clock in the morning, in Lady Dodds-Freeman's flat, with her head bashed in by one of the old lady's gin-bottles.

The £5,000 was missing.

Also by Frank Parrish in Sphere Books:

SNARE IN THE DARK
BAIT ON THE HOOK

Face at the Window

FRANK PARRISH

SPHERE BOOKS LIMITED
London and Sydney

First published in Great Britain by
Constable and Company Limited 1984

Published by Sphere Books Ltd 1986
30–32 Gray's Inn Road, London WC1X 8JL

TRADE
MARK

Printed and bound in Great Britain by
Cox & Wyman Ltd, Reading

I

The Monk's House, Medwell Fratrorum, was supposed in the village to have been something to do with the Priory. This was not a very satisfactory theory, because the house was nowhere near the Priory; perhaps it had belonged to a man called Monk. Latterly, and as long as anybody could remember, it had belonged to old Mr Lambrick. The house sat like a spider in its two hundred acres, and old Mr Lambrick sat like a spider in the house.

It was the one considerable place in the area which Dan Mallett never went near. Dan – odd-job man to the nobility and gentry, clown, leprechaun, survivor of a vanished age, quaint vestige in his rural rock-pool – never went anywhere where the work was hard or the pay was low. With old Mr Lambrick the work would have been very hard and the pay very low. Dan was also depressed by the ugliness of the Victorian house and the squalor of the neglected garden. There was nothing there for him. Since there were no pheasants in the bit of wood, the place was no more beguiling by night than by day. It was a waste of what should have been a centre of lavishness.

Then old Mr Lambrick died. The executors sold nearly all the land to two local farmers, and the house and garden to a developer. There was not much the developer could do, owing to the supposed historical associations of the house; he could neither demolish nor externally alter. He could internally alter, and he did what most of the village considered sensible if a little lowering: he converted the house into three substantial flats.

Dan Mallett watched and listened, throughout the process of conversion. He did not involve himself, because the builder's men worked pretty hard. He saw rewiring and replumbing, and new doors and partitions and cupboards. After a time all these things would begin to bend, fray, come adrift; lights would fuse, loos flood, doors stick. The people who had come to live in the flats would ask about locally for a man to fix things. The local nobs would recommend Dan, saying that he was priceless, hardly believable, too funny for words, straight out of Thomas Hardy, and so forth. This was because the air and accent he put on for the nobs *was* straight out of Thomas Hardy, a parody of old, slow Wessex dialect that always seemed to him grotesquely overdone. But the nobs lapped it up. In the fullness of time, the new nobs in the Monk's House would lap it up. Then there would be gentle tinkering jobs with long, long tea-breaks; then there would be an appraisal of rugs, silver, clocks, the discreet sale of which would add to the slow-growing, ever-growing fund for the operation on his mother's arthritic hip.

The work was finished; the flats were inspected, sold, and presently occupied. Still Dan listened and watched. Now everybody else was listening and watching, too, but Dan was the least obtrusive and most attentive witness.

There was good news and bad.

The good news was Sir David and Lady Dodds-Freeman, who were old and rich and hospitable and had much the best flat. They were childless; they were inseparable; they had a superb collection of early Georgian silver. They had a sophisticated burglar alarm and double-locking windows.

The moderately bad news was in the second-best flat: two widowed sisters who had joined forces, Mrs Gwyneth Addison and Mrs Erica Heron, who lived daintily but sparsely, and who had Benares brass rather than Georgian silver. Mrs Addison had married daughters in places like Brisbane and Bangkok. Mrs Heron had a son who sometimes skidded up in a sports car; he was called Guy, and he worked in advertising. Word in the village was that he was a problem, but he was not a problem Dan had any interest in solving.

The third-best flat had the third-best occupants: Mr Aidan Winfrey and his wife Rose. He was loud and tweedy; he played golf; he was an obtrusive bore in the Chestnut Horse. He was a semi-retired marketing consultant. His wife was semi-retired, too, to a chaise-longue on which she lay softly complaining about how uncomplaining she was. Word got about that she had a bad heart and a good bank-balance. The men in the pub and the women in the shop said he had never made any money; when he went to London on business, two days once a fortnight, she gave him the money for the ticket.

The pickings for Dan were unexpectedly lean. Mr Winfrey, reckoned good with his hands, did all the odd jobs and repairs in his own flat and the widows' flat. He did his own section of the garden. Mrs Heron and Mrs Addison, in big hats, did their bit of the garden. Only from Sir David and Lady Dodds-Freeman did the expected bounty flow. Unfortunately, Sir David was far more intelligent than the run of local nobs. Dan was aware of amusing him, but not of taking him in. When he paid money he wanted value for money; he was not going to be fobbed off with antique rural proverbs, or a performance out of *Under the Greenwood Tree*. He told Dan what to do in the garden, and then came and made sure he had done it. It was not at all what Dan was used to. Lady Dodds-Freeman would have been a far softer touch, if Dan could have got her alone, but she never was alone. Dan admitted that it was touching, a couple so elderly still so devoted to one another; but it was a perfect nuisance.

The Georgian silver was inaccessible, and probably too hot for Dan to handle.

The Dodds-Freemans had outlived nearly all their friends; the few that remained were remote or bedridden. They made new friends locally, but they were really too grand for the village. Their conversation revealed long-ago friendships in the higher aristocracy, weekends at stately homes, suites at Claridges. The nobs and near-nobs whose conversations Dan overheard became resentful; they thought they were being patronized when they were asked to drinks on Sunday morning; but they always went when they were asked, in case anybody should think they were not asked. Dan recognized the whole syndrome, from memories of the hated days of his peonage in the bank in Milchester: the blokes who had drinks with the manager in the pub after work, and the blokes who didn't. It was a thing to be seen doing; it was a thing not to be seen not doing. Dan despaired of most of human nature.

And still, with unceasing bitterness, his mother despaired of him. The bank had been her idea. With his grammar-school education, and the posh accent he could adopt when need arose, he could have lived a life of little black shoes and big blond desks; married a nice little wife, daughter of a solicitor or an accountant; lived in a nice little house on the edge of Milchester, with golden privet round the gravel and a shiny car in the garage . . . Almost, almost, Dan had allowed himself to be prodded down that dreadful road. Then his father had died, as secretly as he had lived, after spending a night in a wet ditch under the boots of the gamekeepers: and Dan had inherited a couple of shotguns, four working dogs, an infinity of lines, wires, loops, nets, pegs, and other instruments for removing game from the preserves of the pampered: and Dan had rediscovered in himself a deep need to live his father's life, with his nose close to the ground and the sky over his head, associate of animals instead of bank-clerks, servant of his own decision or caprice instead of a manager's . . . and he had broken his mother's heart, and it was still unmended. Dan felt very badly about it: but not so badly that any inducement on earth would have sent him back into servitude.

Sir David Dodds-Freeman was exactly the opposite. He had hated retiring from the industrial giant of which he had been chairman. He had too little to do. He was not a man who had hobbies, and he was too old to travel. He pruned roses, but did no other gardening. He sometimes cooked elegant little meals for himself and his wife. Dan saw these meals; he would have eaten both helpings himself, and then wondered what was for lunch. Sir David clung to his wife, it seemed to Dan, simply because he had nothing better to do. He inspected Dan's efforts in the garden for the same reason. Truth to tell, it was for the same reason that he mixed Sunday morning martinis for the local nobs, which they swallowed and enjoyed and resented.

Then Sir David died, suddenly, in the early morning. The village thought his widow would sell the big, luxurious flat and move away, maybe to London, or to one of the south-coast towns where there was company for such as her. But she stayed. After fifty-three years of marriage – after the years of his retirement when they had done everything together, twenty-four hours a day – she missed him dreadfully. But she bore up pretty well. She went about less. Fewer people came for drinks, fewer and fewer, until she stopped asking anybody. When anybody called, the vicar or the man to read the electricity meter, there was a quick movement, as of something being hidden behind a curtain or under a cushion.

At first she only drank wine, as she had all through her married life. Then she discovered the superior analgesia of gin.

Dan knew about it long before anybody else did. He was full of pity, and of disgust. He had never known a drunken old lady before. He did not tell anybody but inevitably it got known, known and most ruthlessly talked about. As the months went by, the village was full of stories – how Lady Dodds-Freeman had been found by her cleaning-woman in a drunken stupor in the kitchen in the middle of the morning, how PC Gundry had found her wandering in the churchyard at midnight, falling over the gravestones and calling for a dog she did not have.

Opinion among the other residents of the Monk's House was divided. Aidan Winfrey took a bluff, man-of-the-world view, expounded boisterously in the Chestnut Horse – if the old girl could afford the stuff, and it deadened the pain of her bereavement, then why the hell not? Rose, his wife, was frightened in case the old lady set the house on fire. Mrs Gwyneth Addison was compassionate, although her own widowhood had been attended by no such excesses; she put it all down to loneliness; she visited her unfortunate neighbour constantly, out of pure kindness, until Lady Dodds-Freeman told her thickly to go away and stay away. Mrs Erica Heron was shocked, and said so loudly and often. Young Mr Guy Heron, hearing all about it at wearisome length whenever he visited his mother, was totally indifferent.

Dan continued to look after the garden, one morning a week, but he went by the Monk's House more often than that. Lady Dodds-Freeman's condition had become locally notorious, and word must have spread to back-street pubs in Milchester. The collection of silver was also well known. The burglar alarm, an obtrusive red cube over the front door of the flat, was no longer a deterrent: the old lady had never understood how to work it, and she was now too confused and incompetent to learn. She was always tiddly by mid-afternoon, and usually dead drunk by ten. Dan kept an eye on her. He became aware that PC Gundry was keeping an eye on her too, which was the first time Dan and the local police had ever acted in harmony.

Rose Winfrey and Mrs Heron, separately and jointly, tried to get Lady Dodds-Freeman's doctor to put her in a home. Dan thought this was a sneaky kind of carry-on, but he also thought the idea a good one. The doctor thought it was a bad one. Lady Dodds-Freeman had acquired the cunning of the drunkard. She always saw her doctor first thing in the morning; she was always sane, sober, and fairly clean. She was entitled to be unsteady on her legs – she was in her middle seventies. The conspiracy failed. There was quite a row, witnessed by Dan among the roses, between the widowed sisters, about it all. Dan was not intentionally eavesdropping; at least, he could pretend that he was not; he just happened to be doing something to Lady Dodds-Freeman's roses, and Mrs Addison and Mrs Heron were near the boundary between their garden and hers.

'She deserves compassion,' said Mrs Addison. 'If she is doing any harm to anybody, it is only herself.'

'You do not seem to understand *true* compassion,' said Mrs Heron. 'You never did. That is probably why your children live at the other end of the world. Is a surgeon less compassionate or more compassionate, doing an operation to save somebody's life?'

Dan, thinking of his mother, saw the force of Mrs Heron's argument.

The ladies saw Dan. They realized that he had heard and understood; it was no good pretending they had been discussing something quite different. Each tried to enlist Dan on her side, which was purposeless but, in Dan's experience, normal.

To Mrs Addison and Mrs Heron, as to all other nobs, Dan adopted the treacly rural accent which made them trust him. He twisted his cap in his hands, blinked his bright blue eyes shyly at them, and tried to think of something quaint and homespun.

'A-do b'lieves,' he said at last, 'her leddyship ben nex' kin t'sickly.'

'Just what I say!' said Mrs Heron. 'It would be kinder to have her properly looked after.' Mrs Heron was a chunky woman approaching sixty, who looked as though she might herself have been a hospital matron. If so, she would have stood no nonsense from alcoholic old ladies.

'Ay, but,' said Dan, having no wish to antagonize Mrs Addison, 'A-do b'lieves her ben mezzerable, leaven thicky house wi' all they memories.'

'My point precisely,' said Mrs Addison. 'To be cruel to be kind is one thing. To be cruel to be cruel is quite another.'

'I think that was supposed to be an epigram,' said Mrs Heron, as though confidentially, to Dan.

'Hum,' said Dan, pretending not to know what an epigram was.

'A remark is no less valid for being well-expressed,' said Mrs Addison.

Dan thought this true enough, though put in a fancy way. It was typical of Mrs Addison. If her sister was like an ex-matron, she was like an ex-schoolmistress, five years older, stringy, crop-haired, tending to be highbrow, a reader of learned magazines. They both had prominent grey eyes and strong chins: otherwise you would never have guessed they were sisters.

Dan thought it a good moment for proverbial philosophy. He invented one of the antique adages the nobs liked. 'There do be times,' he said, 'when folks as disagrees ben like sexton an' bricklayer.'

Mrs Heron smiled interrogatively. She was more impressed by Dan's proverbs than her sister was.

'Sexton ben usen a big spade, for t'dig down,' explained Dan. 'Brickie, he ben usen a liddle spade for to build up. They ben differ as can be, and there ben no road t'draw they nigh.'

At this moment Mrs Sawyer, who cleaned the big flat for Lady Dodds-Freeman, came out of the house and crossed the lawn towards the sisters. Her continued employment had been a surprise and a relief to the other residents: at least the place was clean. Mrs Sawyer's attitude to the empty bottles was that she put them in the dustbin: that was the end of her responsibility in the matter. She was never there in the afternoon, so she only saw her employer a little drunk. She was paid well above the local going rate, and she took home plenty of expensive leftovers.

'That's it,' said Mrs Sawyer, calling out because she was still some distance away. 'That's me lot. Never again. Accused o' pilferen summat she up an' gave me.'

'She will have forgotten all about it tomorrow, Mrs Sawyer,' said Mrs Addison.

'I won't ha' forgot about it,' said Mrs Sawyer. 'Not tomorrer nor never. Not if she got on her bended knees.'

Mrs Sawyer's huge red face showed an anger which would be permanent. She was the unforgiving type. She stumped away to get her bicycle.

'She will have to find a replacement,' said Mrs Addison.

'She?' said Mrs Heron. 'She can't find her own bedroom, let alone a competent cleaner we can all trust. Even you must admit, Gwyneth, that this strengthens my argument.'

'It does nothing of the kind. At best it gives you another excuse for cruelty. You made just now a wounding and offensive reference to my daughters. They live where they do because they are dutiful wives, having been brought up with morality and propriety. Better for us all if your son lived far away. You might then be able to afford your share of the housekeeping.'

This should not have been said in front of Dan. He knew it as well as both ladies. Embarrassed, he addressed himself with passionate concentration to pruning a rose. Mrs Heron walked away. The back of her head looked angry.

'You will please forget my last remark, Mallett,' said Mrs Addison.

'Never did hear un proper,' said Dan. 'Ben forgot afore 'twas said.'

Strenuous efforts were made over the next few weeks to find a new daily for Lady Dodds-Freeman. But the village women wanted nothing to do with the job. Mrs Sawyer's resentment had not lost in the frequent telling; none of the women wanted to be called thieves, especially not those who were thieves. The trouble was, as Dan understood from what he overheard, that any woman who took the job would have been suspected, by the whole village, of doing it for what she could pinch. Nobody wanted that thought of them. It would have been a dreadful loss of face for anybody who replaced Mrs Sawyer. Medwell Fratrorum was too small a place to lose face in. So the flat began to smell, and empty bottles piled up in the spare bedroom.

The problem was solved in a surprising way, and by a completely surprising person. Young Mr Guy Heron came down in his sports-car from London with a small and very pretty girl. Dan, once again among the roses, watched with admiration as the girl got out of the car and crossed the gravel. He thought she moved like a dancer or a gymnast. She wore tight white trousers. She looked very nice in them, and she would have looked very nice without them. There was nothing Dan could do about that. She would probably be gone in an hour or two; and if Guy Heron was the sort of thing she liked, Dan would not be the sort of thing she liked.

All these assumptions turned out to be completely wrong. The girl had a relative in the village, a widowed near-nob called Mrs Young, a mild lady whom Dan scarcely knew. The girl was staying with Mrs Young and had simply accepted a lift from Guy Heron. They were not particular friends; they hardly knew one another. They had met at his advertising agency, at an audition for television commercials, when she was trying to get a job. She was an out-of-work would-be actress, with a diploma from a drama school, and eighteen months of trying to get work. She was taking a rest in the country, to recharge her batteries for the battle. She was called Natasha Chapman. Everybody in the village knew all this almost immediately, because Mrs Young told them.

Equally soon, Natasha Chapman knew all about Lady Dodds-Freeman, the old lady and the young being the two hot topics in the village. Somebody suggested she could make some pocket-money by cleaning the old lady's flat. It might have been Mrs Heron or Mrs Addison; it might have been Aidan Winfrey, hoping that a glamorous little actress in the house might get him a bit of innocent fun. Dan first knew about it when Natasha came out of the house with a cup of tea for him.

'A-do thank ye, liddle missy,' said Dan in his broadest voice.

For the housework she was wearing jeans and an old sweater. There was a smear of grease on her cheek. Her hair was tied up in a scarf. She looked like somebody acting somebody being a cleaning-woman. She looked marvellous. Dan inspected her, smiling his thanks as he took the cup. His smile was not forced or false, but he hoped it might have the effect which, without vanity, he knew it sometimes had. It was a little-boy smile with a bit of lechery.

'A right Augean stable ye ben tacklen yere,' said Dan. It was, of course, ridiculous to use his yokel voice for an allusion to classical mythology. The girl looked at him, completely puzzled. He thought she was intrigued.

He thought he would intrigue her some more. In his banker's voice he said, 'Hercules diverted a river into the stables. Have you considered that?'

'Good gracious,' said Natasha, 'you're a better actor than I am. But which is the performance?'

'It do depand on company, like,' said Dan, once more anciently rural. In his other voice he said, 'Which do you prefer?'

'I like them both,' she said. Her voice was low. She was not putting on any act at all, but she sounded like an actress. She smiled. Her smile was unexpectedly broad; it made her look younger. They stood smiling at one another. Dan allowed more lechery into his smile.

'I hope you'll be here for a bit,' said Dan, making a remark of conventional politeness into all kinds of invitations and suggestions.

'I hope so too,' said Natasha. Her smile disappeared, as though she had suddenly shocked herself by the implications of what she had said. Then her smile reappeared, as though she decided she didn't mind shocking herself.

'I must get back. Not having a river,' she said.

'Alpheus,' said Dan.

'What?'

'The river. I've just remembered the name. Supremely useless information.'

'Why on earth are you working in a garden?'

'Only part of my vocation,' said Dan.

'Oh yes. That policeman says you're the biggest villain unhung.'

'You don't want to believe everything Jim Gundry says.'

'I don't think I want to believe everything you say.'

'No, don't. Pick and choose. Will you believe me if I say you're the most beautiful and desirable girl I've seen for a very long time?'

'I've met fast workers, but this is ridiculous.'

Dan saw a warning light. Natasha was not cross or defensive, but she was also not a fool or a tart. He had gone as far as it was wise to go, in words. It was not the time or place to go anywhere with other than words. Besides, his hands were covered with soil. He smiled, and handed her the empty teacup. She was still smiling as she walked back to the house. He watched her go, admiring the trained, dancer's grace of her movement. She turned in the door. Her smile was still there, and so was his.

The whole scene could have been – doubtless was – witnessed by Mrs Rose Winfrey, and probably by Mrs Addison or Mrs Heron or both. All but one line of it could safely have been overheard. But Dan knew he had met an important new girl, and he knew – with gratitude, without vanity – that he intrigued and attracted her. He had never made love to an actress. He greatly looked forward to doing so.

Mrs Heron went away for a few days to London. Aidan Winfrey went away on one of his fortnightly trips to London. But, as though to make up for these departures, there was a completely unexpected arrival. It was seen, and later described, both by Mrs Addison peering out of her window, and by Rose Winfrey peering out of hers.

The arrival was a tubby, middle-aged man in a small Ford van. There was another man with him, younger. They rang Lady Dodds-Freeman's bell, and she let them in. Neither Dan nor Natasha was there – Natasha came only three days a week, and Dan one day. After a short time, the younger man came out of the house. He got from the van a flat, expensive-looking object that Mrs Addison thought was a radio and Mrs Winfrey a tape-recorder. He took it into the house. He took from the van into the house a number of large cardboard boxes. From the way he carried them it was obvious they were empty.

Mrs Addison was suspicious. She wrote down the number of the van.

Mrs Winfrey was suspicious. She telephoned PC Gundry. He was out. She left a message with his wife.

The younger man came out of the house with his cardboard boxes. He carried them one by one. It was obvious that they were now full.

The older man came out, escorted by Lady Dodds-Freeman. It was mid-afternoon, so she was drunk but not incapable. The man was carrying the radio or tape-recorder; Lady Dodds Freeman was carrying a large brown envelope. The van drove away. Lady Dodds-Freeman waved, and the men waved to her from the van.

Mrs Addison, by her own report, was curious and worried. Lady Dodds-Freeman had not been harmed. She seemed unusually cheerful. It was not robbery with violence, but it might be a kind of robbery. Mrs Addison had heard of the doorstep dealers who gave lonely old people a little money for a lot of money's worth. It was shocking, but not illegal. Mrs Addison wanted to reassure herself, but she had been snubbed so often. She decided it was her duty to risk a snub.

She was not snubbed, she was welcomed. Lady Dodds-Freeman was cock-a-hoop. She showed Mrs Addison what was in the envelope: £5,000 in cash.

She had sold all the Georgian silver, worth at least £100,000. Mrs Addison could not make her understand that she had been cheated; she waved her sheaves of banknotes in boozy triumph, promising herself dozens of cases of gin.

PC Gundry arrived on his bicycle. He was appalled but powerless. From Lady Dodds-Freeman's ramblings it could be deduced that the electrical object was a tape-recorder, and into it the old lady had been induced to say that she was entering with full understanding and agreement into an arrangement with the dealer, and that she was quite satisfied with the price she was being paid.

PC Gundry tried to take the money away from her, to put it in the safe in his cottage. She would not be parted from it. She crooned over the banknotes, cradling them. She wailed when she dropped some. Only by violence would she be separated from them.

Mrs Addison spoke to her sister in London with the news. Rose Winfrey spoke to her husband in London with the news.

PC Gundry told his wife Beryl, who told a few other people, so that half an hour after the Chestnut Horse opened the whole village knew.

The Milchester police traced the van to a firm called Heritage Antiques Ltd. Yes, their Mr Blunt had visited Lady Dodds-Freeman. They could not say how he had heard about the collection of silver. They could say that the whole transaction had been amicable; it had been entirely legal, and this could be proved by a tape-recording.

Dan met Natasha, only their third meeting. He was not quite such a fast worker: it was necessary to avoid crudity or the appearance of overconfidence. He kissed her: he could now safely go that far. She told him the news.

They went round to the Monk's House. Lady Dodds-Freeman made them boisterously welcome, waving handfuls of banknotes. She was pretty drunk now, as it was after seven. Natasha made a grimace at Dan, behind the old lady's back. She hadn't seen her employer in this condition, and she didn't like it. Dan had a sudden and strong desire to kiss that wrinkled button nose. He fought it down. Lady Dodds-Freeman dropped several hundreds of pounds; notes drifted over the carpet. Dan and Natasha both stooped to pick them up. Lady Dodds-Freeman screamed at them, suddenly suspicious, hostile, possessive. She told them thickly to drop the money, to get out of her house.

At this moment PC Gundry came in. He heard Lady Dodds-Freeman screaming that Dan was a thief. PC Gundry stared at Dan, his expression as suspicious and hostile as Lady Dodds-Freeman's.

'She dropped them. We were picking them up,' said Natasha.

'One way o' puttin' it,' said PC Gundry.

Dan and Natasha started to leave, the atmosphere having become inimical. As they were half-way to the door, the telephone rang. Lady Dodds-Freeman started eagerly towards it, but staggered and clutched the back of a chair. PC Gundry picked up the telephone. It was for him: his wife telling him that he was needed.

'Bloke's broke another bloke's head wi' a bottle?' repeated

PC Gundry to the telephone. 'Car-park o' the Chestnut Horse? Herm. I'll be there.'

He shooed Dan and Natasha out of Lady Dodds-Freeman's flat, flapping his arms, like a man shooing geese out of a farmyard.

'Git away from there an' stay away, Dan Mallett,' he said.

'Somebody ought to be there,' said Natasha.

'Leave it to the law, miss. I'll be back.'

'Good,' said Dan, to PC Gundry's visible surprise.

'That was horrible,' said Natasha.

'Depressing,' said Dan. 'Rapid downhill slide.'

He put his arm round her, as they walked back to Mrs Young's cottage. The purpose of the arm was to comfort her. The chance for anything else had been lost, for the moment; the mood was broken. The arm did comfort her; so did Dan's parting kiss, which was moderately lecherous, and to which she responded passionately but briefly.

'Come in for a bit,' said Natasha. 'Cousin Edith won't mind.'

'Can't, dammit,' said Dan. 'Urgent business appointment.'

'At this time of night?'

Dan nodded, smiling apologetically.

'Of course, I was forgetting,' said Natasha. 'You're the biggest villain unhung.'

She thereupon kissed him, an initiative she had not previously taken. It was another brief embrace, but Dan was pleased. He liked this girl very much. She was ambitious without toughness, talented without conceit, strongly moral (in some directions) without priggishness, astonishingly ignorant without stupidity. She was not quite like anything he had met.

He was not in the least like anything she had met, in a middle-class suburb and then in Chelsea and Fulham. She went indoors unaware of the width of her smile. If Dan had come in, she thought, he would not have been able to stay long. Natasha herself had a business appointment, astonishing as this would have seemed to anybody in the village. It was not something she was ashamed of – not much, anyway – but it was not something for Cousin Edith to know about, or PC Gundry, or anybody in Medwell Fratrorum. Not even Dan. Least of all Dan.

The car came for her at eight, with Laurence Catchpole at the wheel. They drove into Milchester. Cousin Edith thought they were simply going out to dinner, and was innocently pleased on her young relative's account. They went to a chalet Laurence had taken at the Wessex Motor Inn. They would be at it most of the night. It had to be night, because Laurence was kept busy all day by the *Milchester Argus* and at weddings and receptions and school sports. He was a photographer. Natasha was posing for him, in the nude, with a variety of props, for a calendar for the local brewery. Laurence was moonlighting. It was a big break for him professionally, but his wife would have forbidden it and the *Argus* would have sacked him, if they knew. It was good money for Natasha, who had left many unpaid bills in London. She was not frightened of Laurence. He was a decent little man, struggling like everybody else to hoist himself up a bit. (Like everybody else except Dan.) But from everybody's point of view it was a thing to keep very, very quiet about.

Natasha peeled in the chalet's tiny bathroom. She came shyly out to face Laurence's lights and his lens. For January she wore a woolly cap (nothing else) and held a pair of skis. They had a long, exhausting and totally innocent night, punctuated by instant coffee.

Dan went home to get his mother's supper and his own, and that of his dogs, bantams and fancy pigeons. They sat down at eight to a rich and savoury stew of unbought ingredients. Dan felt a wrench in his heart, comparing the face that looked at him over the table with the one he had kissed an hour before. Natasha's was smooth as a peach, pink-gold from the midsummer sun, dewy with youth, shining with health. His mother's, once as berry-brown as his own, was now like crumpled white tissue-paper; it seemed to him that every time he looked there were new lines, and that they were lines of pain. And some of them were lines of disappointment and betrayal, at the life he had chosen and the runagate he was.

He cleared away and washed up, and put his mother to bed. He did not say that he was going out. He did not need to. She always knew.

'Ye thieven or wenchen?' she asked, as she usually did, in a voice at once martyred and accusing. She had not lost hope of his reformation, of his return to little black shoes and big green filing-cabinets.

Dan smiled, non-committally. It was no good lying to her, and no good telling the truth either.

'Good-night, old lady,' he said.

'Goo'night, ye liddle villain,' she said, her voice full of disapproval and of love.

He went out quietly, disturbing the dogs as little as possible in order to disturb her as little as possible. He crossed the country, disdaining roads like a fox, without light or sound or any hesitation or the appearance of haste. He went to Major Coxen's field, two hundred yards from the Coxens' house, and to the padlocked gate. He opened the padlock with the key Major Coxen had given him, groped for and found the leather head-collar and the halter-rope which the Major had left for him, hidden by the gate. He located the big bay thoroughbred Snapdragon, put the halter on him, and led him out of the field. He shut the gate behind him, to keep in the other horses, but left the padlock undone. He led the horse to a box which was waiting on the Igton road. It was a long way, but the place had been chosen for safety. Snapdragon did not want to go for a long walk at night, led by a strange man to a strange place. Dan did not care to ride a strange horse, bareback, at night, especially a young thoroughbred full of grass. Dan and the box-driver at last loaded Snapdragon into the box, and the box drove away. It was going to a dealer at the other end of England.

The horse had been a present to Major Coxen's daughter Diana from her godfather, for her eighteenth birthday. He meant it as a point-to-pointer, and so did she. She intended to school and train him herself, qualify herself, and ride the races herself. She was absolutely clear about this; she was adamant about it. She had been spoiled all her life by her mother and she always got her own way. Her father knew that she had not the knowledge to school a young horse to jump fences at speed, and she had not the skill or strength to ride in a steeplechase. She shouted him down, with quiet shouts, when he said so. He succeeded, like so many fathers in similar predicaments, only in increasing her determination.

So Major Coxen paid Dan Mallett to steal his daughter's horse. He himself was safely away, staying with his brother in Cheshire.

Dan was surprised to find himself doing something both legal and morally admirable. But it would not have done for a whisper of the transaction to get out. Major Coxen's life was miserable enough as it was. He trusted Dan, which was also, for Dan, a surprising and gratifying experience. Also, Major Coxen's payment, which was generous, was conditional on everything going without a hitch.

Dan got back to his cottage, the one-time gamekeeper's cottage under the dripping edge of the Priory Woods, when the sky was growing pale and the birds were getting busy. He was bottomlessly tired. But it was a merit of his way of life that, if he chose, he could spend all morning in bed.

Not that morning. He was woken by his mother, after what seemed like one minute. With her was a policeman in uniform, strange to Dan. He was to come along. He was to give an account of his movements the previous night. He had immediate and sickening visions of having been seen taking the horse.

The reality was even more sickening. Mrs Gwyneth Addison, neighbour of old Lady Dodds-Freeman, had been found by PC Gundry at nine o'clock in the morning, in Lady Dodds-Freeman's flat, with her head bashed in by one of the old lady's gin-bottles.

The £5,000 was missing.

2

Lady Dodds-Freeman had been in a deep and drunken slumber, from perhaps ten o'clock. Her own accounts of her bedtime varied, between barely credible limits. She would have seen and heard nothing. Mrs Erica Heron was away in London, as was her son Guy. Mr Aidan Winfrey was away in London. His wife Rose had gone to bed with a Mogadon at half-past ten. PC Gundry had not been able to get back to the Monk's House after the fracas at the Chestnut Horse.

Hundreds of people knew that Lady Dodds-Freeman was drunk every night. Hundreds of people knew that she had £5,000 in cash in her flat. It was entirely obvious that one of those hundreds had broken into the flat, that Mrs Addison had heard something and investigated, and that the burglar had used, on her poor old head, the nearest available weapon.

There were no fingerprints on the bottle. It had been wiped, though a small amount of blood and hair still stuck to it. It had been wiped with a dishcloth from the kitchen, which had been dropped on the floor beside the body. The dishcloth carried no fingerprints.

There were no signs of forcible entry. PC Gundry had made sure the front door was locked when he left to go to the pub, therefore Lady Dodds-Freeman must have left a window open; the burglar must have used it, closed it once he was in, and unlocked the front door from inside, so that Mrs Addison, investigating, had found it unlocked. It seemed improbable that Mrs Addison had climbed in through the window, though she was a vigorous lady and it was possible. It seemed improbable that Lady Dodds-Freeman had admitted the burglar through the front door, though it was possible that she had done so and then, drunk, had forgotten about it. Another possibility was that the burglar had had a key. There had almost certainly been spare front-door keys, but none was found in the flat. Lady Dodds-Freeman did not know how many keys there had been, or what had become of them.

Mrs Sawyer the ex-cleaning-lady admitted having had a key, but said that she had left it behind on the kitchen table the day she departed in a rage. Natasha Chapman denied having seen this key or any other key, except the one on Lady Dodds-Freeman's ring. None of the other surviving residents of the flats admitted to having keys to Lady Dodds-Freeman's flat, and there was no reason why Mrs Addison should have had one. Dan Mallett said he had never had a key. The key left by Mrs Sawyer on the kitchen table, if in truth it had been, could have been seen and taken by anybody going into the flat in the weeks between her departure and the night of the murder. This included an unknown number of deliverymen from the grocer, wine merchant, butcher, fishmonger; men to read meters or fix things; an unknown number – perhaps nil – of local snoopers; the men from Heritage Antiques who had taken the silver; Mrs Heron; Mrs Addison herself; Aidan Winfrey; Natasha Chapman; Dan Mallett.

Everybody who knew about the money had a motive for the burglary. Nobody would not be better off with £5,000 in untraceable used banknotes. Interruption of the burglary was sufficient motive for the murder. Some of the people who knew about the money would have wanted it more badly than others: it was well known to the police, for example, that Dan Mallett wanted a lot of money for an operation on his mother's arthritic hip, because she refused to have anything to do with the National Health. And some of the people who knew about the money would have been better at hitting Mrs Addison on the head with a gin-bottle: it was thought that Dan Mallett, though small, would have been very good at that. It was thought that he would have gone to extreme lengths to avoid being caught in a crime; though prison would not kill him, his going to prison would kill his mother: she would be institutionalized, and she would die of rage. Everybody knew all this.

To the police Dan used a somewhat moderated version of his antique rural manner. His old acquaintance the Detective Chief

Superintendent from Milchester (the one who looked like a fox) became impatient with homespun proverbs.

'A-ben out an' about 'at night,' Dan said, 'a sight o' miles from Monk's. A-bent at liberty t' tell ye where or wi' oo. A-ben worken for a gent, right an' tight an' legal, but all ben confidential.'

They did not believe him, but there was no way that, with what they knew, they could cobble together a case to put in front of a jury. They let him go with a visible reluctance which he thought in bad taste.

His mother tried to hide her joy when he came back safe and hungry.

Natasha treated him with a sort of wariness. When he would not tell her where he had gone after he had put his mother to bed, she looked at him, frowning. People had been talking to her, including the police. They knew that Dan and she both worked part-time for Lady Dodds-Freeman, and consequently knew one another. They knew both had seen the money tumbling out of the old lady's arms. They told her about the expensive operation Dan's mother needed. She knew, from Dan himself, how much he worried about his mother's arthritis. He tried to kiss away her suspicions, but she did not respond as she had done two days before. He continued to intrigue her, but now he also frightened her. He saw that she saw him as something from a different, wild, primeval world. He had the blood of hundreds of wild creatures on his hands; why not of a person also? There was still witchcraft in the countryside (she told him she had read so); there were feuds, bloodsports, bloodlust, strange doings under the full moon, a whole world of secret savagery unknown to people in cities. All this, Dan saw, was part of Natasha's attitude to himself. She was fascinated and frightened; she was aloof and withdrawn.

It was a terrible pity. It put his plans back days, even weeks; it might put her out of his reach for good. That was an awful waste. The more he looked at her the more he wanted her, and the more he talked to her the more he liked her. But she was finding it possible to believe, as much of the village believed, that he might be a thief and a murderer.

The police believed it too, and they were working hard at

trying to prove it. Dan wished Major Coxen would come back from Cheshire.

Diana Coxen had reported the theft of her valuable horse. She evidently expected the police of the whole West Country to drop everything and find it. She was not pleased to be told that Snapdragon had probably gone straight to a knacker's, and was probably now in cans of petfood. She was not pleased that a murder investigation preoccupied the local police.

Major Coxen did not come back, but Mrs Heron had of course been summoned immediately her whereabouts were ascertained. It took a police clerk all morning, with an address book found in the Monk's House flat. She was house-sitting in Battersea for a friend who was away in Cornwall; she had intended to be there for ten days. She was required to identify the body, although the whole village could have identified the body. She was supported by her son Guy, who seemed unusually solemn and respectable. Mrs Heron was brave, more than ever like a hospital matron.

Least touched by the shocking episode, of anybody in the area, was Lady Dodds-Freeman. She had her little drink as usual. She had forgotten her rage with Dan and Natasha, and continued to employ both. She sometimes seemed to be searching her flat, but it was not obvious whether she was searching for her silver or her money.

A girl called Sharron Syme went into the village shop. She worked all week as a hairdresser in Milchester. She looked like a hairdresser, a little overweight and very clean. She was a bit stuck up, more popular with men than girls.

She said she had been in the village on the night of the murder, not knowing it was the night of any murder. She had passed the Monk's House at about eleven, on her way to an appointment. She had been visiting her mother, because her auntie was there on a flying visit, and her appointment was with a gentleman with a car, a friend who was giving her a lift back to Milchester. Never mind which friend. They had had a minor accident. She had suffered slight concussion. Nothing serious, but she'd had to spend two days in bed, in the dark, on the flat of her back. Having done so, she was fine. But having done so, she had not seen a paper or listened to the radio or watched the telly. She came back into the world to hear about poor Mrs Addison. It had been a worse shock than the accident.

For she had seen somebody at the door of Lady Dodds-Freeman's flat that night. The person had been looking in through the window beside the front door. Not Mrs Addison, somebody else. It seemed to Sharron Syme that she had seen the murderer.

Sharron was induced, by the women in the shop, to go round at once to PC Gundry. She did not want to go, because she had to catch the bus into Milchester. Her public duty, they said, came before her duty to the hairdresser. Sharron told PC Gundry that her gentleman friend was called Henry. She did not know his other name. His car was a Ford, pale-coloured. She did not know which pale colour, because she only saw the car in the dark. He was not a local man. He came from Manchester or Doncaster. These details were taken down so that the story could be checked; they made it impossible for the story to be checked, but there was no reason why Sharron should have made up any of it.

Sharron gave PC Gundry the description she had already given to the village women. It was not the world's best description – the only light on Lady Dodds-Freeman's front door had been that from Mrs Rose Winfrey's window above, and Sharron had been quite a long way away – but it dramatically narrowed the list of suspects.

Coming away at twelve-thirty from Lady Dodds-Freeman's, Natasha Chapman was aware of some very odd looks. She passed several women she knew by sight, on her way to her cousin Edith Young's. She called 'Good morning', and they looked away quickly. Or they stared, stopped in their tracks and stared, as though at a monster or a freak. Natasha peered at her reflection, in the window of a parked car, wondering if she had some extraordinary smear of grease across her face. Her face was pretty clean; she thought she looked pretty nice, and much as usual. A young woman with a child hurried the child across the road, out of Natasha's way. Natasha was puzzled and annoyed.

Her cousin, when she got home, was twittering with outrage. She had gone into the village shop, unnoticed by some women who were there. The women were clustered in a circle, like the huddle of American footballers before a play. But Mrs Young had heard them.

A small female person, in jeans or trousers, with long fair hair, had been seen at the window of Lady Dodds-Freeman's flat late on the night of the murder.

There were other small young females with long fair hair in the village, many of whom doubtless knew about Lady Dodds-Freeman and about the money. But all of them were probably safe at home, or could be otherwise accounted for. Anyway they were the village's own girls, good girls, kind to old ladies, not ones to steal a lot of money, not ones to bash Mrs Addison on the head with a gin-bottle.

That London girl worked for the old lady. There could only be one reason for her to do that, as the village had agreed weeks before – she was on the nick for what she could get. She knew the old lady better than anybody, working right there in the flat, or pretending to work. She had obviously had a key, and since then had thrown it away and pretended she never had one. She had seen the money – actually handled it. Tried to pinch some of it earlier, seemingly. With that Dan Mallett. She had been seen with him. That was incriminating enough, all by itself. Probably they were in it together. Probably he had done the actual bashing, and they had split the money between the two of them.

Well, if not, where had Natasha Chapman been that night? And where had Dan Mallett been that night?

Dan heard it all from Lady Simpson, who had heard it from her daily, who had heard it in the shop. Dan was gently mowing the Simpsons' lawn; he cut the machine when Lady Simpson came out to him, as many of the nobs magnanimously did, with a cup of tea. She stayed to give him the hot news.

Lady Simpson could never believe ill of Dan Mallett, whom

she regarded as a kind of mascot, a domesticated Cornish imp. She was very ready to believe ill of a snip from London who called herself an actress and never did any acting.

Dan knew Sharron Syme. For a short time, some years previously, he had known her very well indeed. She was obliging, a bit monotonous, and greedy. They had parted amicably and remained, on the rare occasions when they met, on pretty good terms. Dan thought that, in Milchester, she had become a bit of a tart and a bit of a climber. He had no objections to tarts and climbers, but it was not his cup of tea.

The concussion might have been a phoney: Sharron might have been holed up in a motel with a generous travelling salesman. It made no difference. What mattered was what she had seen.

Hideous as it was to face, what she'd seen sounded terribly like Natasha. Natasha had steadily refused to say where she was that night. She had consistently said, as Dan himself had said, that she had a watertight alibi but for personal reasons would only declare it, and produce her witness, if she was actually in the dock. Dan had felt sick, speculating where Natasha might have been all night, and with whom. He had no right to jealousy; she was not his property and never would be. He had no claims on her. She had no obligations of fidelity; she and Dan were not lovers: not even old friends. Dan was the last person to take any posture about morality. Even so, his guesses made him feel sick.

He felt much sicker now. He faced the fact that he really knew nothing about Natasha, though he had been telling himself he did. She was as strange to him as he to her. London was a horribly violent place, where people knocked you on the head and robbed you as soon as look at you. Living in such an atmosphere might make anybody callous.

Natasha owed money, and she was out of work.

Dan was not ready to believe that Natasha had robbed Lady Dodds-Freeman and murdered Mrs Addison, but it struck him that, if she hadn't, she was going to have to use her alibi. And part of him didn't want to hear about that, and part was horribly curious.

Natasha sat all afternoon in her cousin's cottage, wondering when PC Gundry would come to arrest her. She felt deeply sorry for Laurence Catchpole. Instead of helping him, as they'd both thought she was doing, she was about to ruin his life. His wife would walk out on him for spending all night with a naked girl, and the newspaper would sack him for moonlighting. He would join Natasha on the dole, and he was too old and too respectable for that.

The telephone rang. It was for her. It was Laurence Catchpole. He had developed his films, made contact prints in black and white, and shown them to the brewery's advertising manager. They were over the moon, really pleased. They had given him some money on account, quite a lot of money. He could now pay Natasha. He wanted to do so as soon as possible, in fairness to her, and out of gratitude for the hard work she had put in. He would drive out from Milchester as soon as it was dark, and park by the churchyard. If she joined him in the car, he could count out the money he owed her.

Natasha was glad to be meeting him after dark. She wanted no more of those averted eyes in the village street. She would have to tell him about the other business, about the dreadful thing she would probably have to do to him. She felt awful at the prospect.

An extraordinary thought suddenly occurred to her. The person Sharron Syme had seen, the small figure with long fair hair, might be Dan Mallett in a wig. He was certainly capable of disguise. Think of those different voices he had. Was he capable not only of theft and murder, but also of framing her?

Natasha went out to meet Laurence Catchpole with her feelings in a tangle. She was happy to be getting her money. She was racked by suspicions of Dan, which one minute seemed ridiculous and the next horribly convincing. She was deeply unhappy at what honesty compelled her to tell Laurence Catchpole, so that he would be prepared for the bomb when it went up.

She walked to the church. His car was there, well away from the streetlight by the lych-gate. She got in. He was elated by the success of his photographs with the brewery, and he was delighted to be paying her so much and so quickly. Natasha was the more appalled at what she was going to have to tell him.

He handed her a thick brown envelope, reminiscent of that in which Lady Dodds-Freeman had been given her money by the dealers.

'Count it, girlie,' said Laurence Catchpole. 'I had a beer before I came, and I've got to use the churchyard for a purpose no churchyard should be used for.'

Natasha nodded. He got out of the car, leaving on the little overhead light so that she could count her earnings, and disappeared into the dark of the churchyard.

Old Ivy Bevan hobbled home from the village hall where the Old Folk met once a week. As always, she was angry. She had been beaten at dominoes, and she had been cheated of her fair share of cake. It was nasty cake, home-made instead of a proper shop one, but still she had a right to her share.

The gossip had been interesting, though, about how that London tart stopping with that Mrs Young had done in that Mrs Addison, and nicked £5,000 from that Lady Summat. Pity they didn't hang them no more. Ivy Bevan would have enjoyed a public execution, especially of that London tart.

She went along the pavement by the wall of the churchyard, passing under the light by the lych-gate. She saw a car parked. Courting couple, likely, up to something disgusting. Ivy Bevan hobbled up to the car, silent in her carpet-slippers. She stooped painfully, to see what disgusting things the couple in the car were at.

Natasha had the notes and the brown envelope in her lap, visible enough in the overhead light. She was half-way through counting when she saw, out of the corner of her eye, a movement outside the window beside her. She glanced out of the car. An old woman with a kind of beard was staring in, her nose almost pressed to the glass. Instinctively, Natasha hid the money in her lap under her forearms. The old face disappeared.

It did not really matter. It was money honestly earned. The

truth about Laurence Catchpole, though horrible for him, fully and innocently explained both her having the money and her counting it in his car.

But of course, without the truth about Laurence Catchpole, her having a lot of money in cash, and counting it in secret in a parked car, *was* damaging in the last degree. It made her look not like a probable thief and murderer, but like a certain one.

She finished counting the money. It was the £200 exactly, as she had known it would be.

Laurence Catchpole came back, and she told him she would need his evidence.

Of course he knew all about the local murder, but not about Sharron Syme. He did not at first take it in that his life was ruined. Natasha thought he was overstating it, but he said that was how it would be – his life was going to be ruined.

He was decent. Speaking with difficulty, he said that if Natasha really was accused of the murder – and he accepted that this began to look highly likely – then he would of course come forward with the truth. She'd be off the hook, but he'd be on it.

Natasha almost began to feel it would be better to be convicted of murder than to do this to somebody.

She tried to comfort him. Getting out of the car, she saw that he was crying, that there were tears on his cheeks and on his spectacles.

Natasha wondered if he could see to drive, at night, with his spectacles puddled with tears.

He started the car. Like most people in the grip of strong emotion, he accelerated too hard and let in the clutch with a jerk. He roared round in a U-turn.

Perhaps he was blinded by terror of the future, perhaps by tears, perhaps by the flare of the oncoming headlights on the tears on his spectacles. The Range Rover was coming fast from the direction of the Chestnut Horse. Somebody in the pub had noticed the time, and was rushing back to avoid a wife's rage. Laurence Catchpole's car swerved right across the road on to the wrong side, into the path of the oncoming Range Rover. There was nothing the driver of the Range Rover could have done. The vehicles met head-on. Laurence Catchpole's tiny little car had no front. The front was smacked backwards into the rest of it, into Laurence. One of the Range Rover's head-lamps was still working; it shone into Laurence's car and showed that he was full of steering-wheel and dashboard. There was no chance that he could come out of that alive. He did not.

The driver of the Range Rover was shaken but unhurt. He gabbled to Natasha, 'You saw it? You did see it? Came right across in front of me. Swerved right across in front of me. You saw it? You're a witness? You did see it?'

'Yes,' said Natasha, stunned by this sudden, atrocious event, by the horrible mangled thing in the car, which had been a nice man and her friend.

She could think of nothing else for a moment; but after a moment the implications came flooding at her.

The driver of the Range Rover was still jabbering half-coherently. Understandably he was in a state of shock. People who had heard the monstrous noise of the crash came running from their houses.

The brewery had the photographs, thought Natasha. Most were unmistakably of her, but they were not dated. They were not the slightest use as an alibi without Laurence Catchpole's evidence. The money she had been seen counting, the money out of a brown envelope, was innocent only with Laurence Catchpole's evidence.

'There she is,' said a woman. 'Ivy Bevan seen 'er wi' a yuge bundle o' money.'

'Collar 'er.'

'Not arf. Citizen's arrest. Murderen bitch.'

Natasha turned and ran. There were dark roads and dark gardens. She was a gymnast, an athlete. She could run faster than the middle-aged village people who chased her. She got away from the cars and bicycles which joined the chase, simply by leaving the road. She ran clear out of the village, in blind panic, just to get away, not beginning to think about the next minute or the next hour but thinking only of getting away from the mob of village people.

She had time to thank God she was wearing sneakers instead of some of her London shoes.

She was pouring with sweat and her breath was rasping in her throat. She stopped. There was silence behind her. She collapsed under a hedge, drawing deep shuddering breaths. She found she was still clutching the envelope of money.

She was smitten by a sense of appalled pity for Laurence Catchpole: not only that he had died so suddenly and violently and uselessly, but also that he had died in a mood of despairing misery. The thought of Laurence's mood at the moment of his death made Natasha burst into tears.

When she began to think about her own predicament, her tears were for herself as well as for Laurence.

3

Natasha knew where Dan Mallett lived. She had not seen the place, but he had described the cottage and its position. He had made it sound like something out of a German fairy story, made of gingerbread, crawling with assorted livestock, and ruled by a hobbling witch. Driving with her cousin, she had passed the mouth of the track which led to the cottage. She could find it in the dark, and the summer night was not very dark.

She felt deeply nervous about going there. She felt like the fly jumping into the web. All he had had to tell her, if he was innocent, was where he had been on the night of the murder. Trying to kiss her instead of telling her was not satisfactory. Probably it had worked with a lot of girls, but this time a murder was involved.

But she could think of nowhere else to go.

She had enough money to go anywhere, but they would find her anywhere. If they found her in Aberdeen or Abergavenny, she would be in worse trouble, because of running away. The thing was not to be found until the truth was; and the place to go for the truth was Dan's cottage. She would make him tell her. She would be able to do that because his mother was there. Natasha pictured herself holding a poker or a spade over Dan's mother's head, and threatening to bring it down unless he told her the truth. It was not a thing she would actually ever do, but she could convince him she was prepared to do it. She would be good at that; she was an actress; she had been trained to snarl like an animal.

She rehearsed herself, as she walked through the soft night towards the Priory Woods.

Old Mrs Mallett wanted her supper, although she was not hungry. Time was, in her active days, she had had an appetite almost like Dan's. Not quite like his – nobody ate as much as he did, small and skinny as he was, it amazed even the lad himself where he put it all – but she used to eat hearty. She burned it up in those days, digging her bit of garden, cutting firewood, looking after her hens and sometimes a pig, cooking and cleaning and washing. There was none of that now, and never would be again. She was resigned to the pain of her arthritic hip, though she bitterly resented her helplessness.

Almost as bitterly as she resented her only child's treachery, leaving the bank and the solid, respectable suburban future, reverting to his Dad's wicked thieving ways, living more by night than by day, running all the time the risk of a gamekeeper's twelve-bore or a bluebottle's handcuffs.

She would liefer have him as he was than not have him. She was frightened for him all the time, as well as angry with him. Being frightened for him made her more angry with him.

She was angry with him now, for being late with her supper. She might not want the food, but she wanted the routine. She had been cheated of the dainty bungalow on the edge of the town for which her soul craved and which had looked, long ago, like coming her way; she was obliged to stay on and on in the crazy old cottage under the edge of the woods; all the more important that they should live decently in any way they could. Punctual meals was part of that, which Dan never could be made to see.

She shifted crossly, reading the local paper by the light of the pressure-lamp. They'd picked up Dan, of course. They picked him up for everything, and quite right too, but they'd let him go, because even they could see he'd never do anything like that. Mrs Mallett had never seen Mrs Addison, or Lady Hit-the-Bottle, or any of the other people mentioned in the paper, but she knew about them from the few old friends who sometimes came to see her.

She knew about the maidie from London, that all the village said had done it. She was a lovely girl, seemingly, pretty as a flower. That being so, Dan knew her. He'd get to know any pretty girl came anywhere near the place, and give them that smile like a little boy needed comforting, and stare at them, innocent as a babe, with those big blue eyes . . . All just like his father. Nobody could resist his father, herself least of all.

Old Mrs Mallett sighed, looking away from the smudgy newspaper into the dark corner of the crowded little kitchen, looking far and far back over the years. She'd been right envied, catching Mallett, by girls from miles around. To the end of his life there were women who envied her. Even after his death, there were women aplenty who envied her that she'd had him. They were right, too, for all he was a poacher and a runagate, for all he'd brought her to live in this hovel under the branches. They were right: and any girl that got young Dan, got him and tied him up and kept him, she'd be envied far and wide too. There were scores had fallen for him, clever little devil that he was. Nobody could blame one of them.

It was time he settled down, and maybe that just might make the difference. A cradle in the house changed the way a man saw things. The important thing was that he found the right girl, or the right girl found him. 'Right' meant a whole lot of things that wouldn't apply in most cases. It meant a girl from a nice background, professional or business, brought up among streets and tidy gardens, ambitious, nice-spoken, lady-like . . .

Mrs Mallett indulged, for the millionth time, her daydream of Dan bringing home a solicitor's daughter, changing back into gentleman's clothes, joining the bank again, having one of those leather briefcases that looked so important. She had not given up hope. While there was breath in her crippled old body, she would not give up trying.

Meanwhile the boy was out and her supper was late.

As usual he had not really told her where he was going. It was a girl somebody had forgotten to lock up, or something movable somebody had forgotten to nail down. She'd hear about it, maybe, when they sent him off to the prison in Milchester, where he might by now have been manager of the bank.

There was a knock on the door, a rare thing after dark.

Glumly, Mrs Mallett supposed it was another policeman, come to take Dan off to prison. As often before, Dan would come home, sniff that there were policemen in the house, and disappear, probably for days, leaving her to feed his dogs and his bantams and his pesky pigeons.

While he was waiting for Dan, the policeman could get her supper. That, too, had happened more than once before.

'Bent locked,' she called out. Her voice was still strong, though none of the rest of her was.

In came not a policeman but a small and very pretty girl. Her hair was untidy and she was wearing trousers, of which Mrs Mallett disapproved. The girl came in nervously. She had been crying. She glanced quickly round all that she could see of the cottage. She was looking for Dan. Mrs Mallett did not recognize the girl. There were dozens of girls nowadays in the village she did not know by sight, though she had known their parents and probably known them as tinies. But it struck Mrs Mallett that this was not a Medwell girl. There were pretty girls in Medwell, no doubt, or Dan would have moved somewhere else, but not in this girl's style. Untidy as she was, in trousers as she was, there was something delicate and ladylike about her. Dan would like her. Dan must already know her and like her, or why was she here?

It suddenly came to Mrs Mallett who the girl was. She was the London girl, the one they all said had done in the poor lady at the Monk's House.

Old Mrs Mallett stared with interest at the girl, never before having seen a murderess. Her eye was still as sharp as a cobra's, for all her pins hardly carried her when she tried to walk.

'I'm sorry to crash in like this,' said the girl. 'You must be Mrs Mallett.'

She was nicely spoken. Her voice was gentle and ladylike. Mrs Mallett had heard ladies talking, in the old days when she got out and about, and there was no mistaking them. People tried to imitate them, to be posh, but there was no mistaking that either.

Nobody with a face and voice like this girl's face and voice would have smashed in an old lady's head with a gin-bottle.

'Ye seeken Dan?' she said.

'Yes. There are things I've simply got to ask him. But I'll get out of your way.'

'I bent got any way. I bide where I'm put. Set down. 'At chair d'wobble, but 'twon't bust.'

The girl sat down, seeming glad to do so. She looked exhausted and miserable.

She said, 'Do you know when Dan will be back?'

'A should 'a ben back an hour sence. Maken me right late for me tea.'

'I can get your tea, if you'll tell me where things are.'

'Nay! They hands bent for fiddlen wi' pots.'

'Yes, they are. I often cook for myself.'

Mrs Mallett was shocked for a moment. But she remembered hearing that many proper ladies now cooked for themselves. It was extraordinary, but she accepted that it was so. She accepted that the dainty maid who had come into her kitchen was capable of frying a few rashers, and probably of some of the fancy cookery Dan went in for.

An idea was born in Mrs Mallett's cunning and ever-hopeful old brain. Fate had made possible something which had never before been possible: she herself could take a hand in the game. She could influence things directly. Always before, everything had happened outside her ken, outside her power to help.

But she had some checking up to do first.

The girl's name sounded to Mrs Mallett like a sneeze, but the nobs were often odd about names.

The girl Natasha put more wood in the stove. She filled a kettle from the tub which Dan had drawn in the morning from the well, and started to melt a knob of dripping in a pan. These humdrum tasks relaxed her. When Mrs Mallett judged she was sufficiently relaxed, she began to ask her questions about herself.

Dan had not told his mother where he was going, because he never did tell her where he was going in the evening. By day it was different. Many of his errands were quite legal, though deplorable enough to the old lady. Even when she correctly guessed that he was going out, at night, with his snares for pheasants or his nets for woodcock, there was no point in talking about it. There was no point in hurting and enraging her, by proclaiming a way of life so different from the one she had planned for him.

That night there was another reason for silence. He had promised not to say a word to anybody. This, as Dan understood that sort of promise, included Natasha and his mother. It might not, ultimately, include the police, but Dan hoped for Major Coxen's sake that he could keep quiet to the police about it too.

Major Coxen had come back from Cheshire. The horse Snapdragon had arrived safely in Yorkshire. It was coming up for sale quite legally, on Major Coxen's instructions, described in the catalogue as 'property of a lady'. Major Coxen would not of course claim on the insurance, though he would pretend to his daughter that he was doing so. He would buy her a new horse with the money Snapdragon fetched, quite a different sort of horse, an eight-year-old or more, thoroughly schooled, a safe conveyance, a horse she could not consider entering in point-to-point races.

Dan met Major Coxen, by arrangement, just after dark. Major Coxen gave Dan a rustling envelope which he said contained £100 in cash. Dan believed him. There was nothing he could immediately do about it, even if he hadn't believed him, because they were meeting in the dark lane by the Coxens' paddocks. They met there because it was a place where Major Coxen had an excuse to be. He was a man whose domestic life required him to have excuses for everything he did.

Dan pocketed the envelope. He said diffidently, in his lowest and slowest, his most disarmingly treacly, rural accents, that he might need the box-driver's evidence. He might need to prove that he was with the horse, by the box, on the Igton road, miles from the Monk's House, at eleven o'clock on the night of the murder. There need be no mention of Snapdragon by name, or of Major Coxen. What Dan therefore wanted was the name of the box-driver, if Major Coxen knew it, or failing that the name of the horse-transport firm the driver worked for. In the dark, that complicated night, Dan had not seen the name of the firm on the horse-box.

Major Coxen panicked. If it came out about the box and about Dan, then it would come out about himself and

Snapdragon. Diana would make his life unendurable. There was more to it than that – things were more complex than Dan could realize. The godfather who had given Diana the horse would be livid too. Major Coxen could not afford to have that particular man livid with him. The reasons were financial; the man was something in the City. Major Coxen pretended that he had forgotten which of the hundreds of horse-transport firms he had employed. He had destroyed any record of the transaction, in case his daughter found it. It would have been sensible to use either a Yorkshire firm or a local one – the same total mileage would have resulted either way. He thought he had used a Yorkshire firm. He could not remember the name of the dealer to whom Snapdragon had gone.

All this was lies, but Major Coxen was far too frightened of his daughter, and of her godfather, to tell Dan anything. If Dan told the police directly about Major Coxen, it would be a ghastly betrayal of trust, of his given word. Major Coxen would flatly deny the whole thing. It would be his word against Dan's. That of a gallant and decorated ex-officer against that of a notorious rogue.

He had a point. But Dan wondered how a man who had won an MC in the Italian campaign could be so frightened of his daughter. Meanwhile nothing he said, in a wheedling voice which had become almost incomprehensible even to himself, made any difference to the Major's attitude. It was better that Dan should go to prison for life, than that those two should know who stole Snapdragon.

The whole thing took far longer than Dan had expected, because of his sustained effort to get one name out of Major Coxen. His mother would be getting highly impatient for her supper, even though, when she got it, she would eat very little of it.

He loped home across country, through the thin midsummer night. The sky was clear. Though there was no moon, he could see almost as well as by day; his night vision was better than other people's because, he supposed, he used it more. In spite of the darkness there was birdsong. Loudest and nearest were sedge-warblers, in the thick vegetation beside the river. His father had called them 'pit-sparrows', sparrow being what he called any small brown bird. Warbler was a rum name too, Dan thought, for a bird with a song like that. Blackbirds warbled. Sedge-warblers chattered, buzzed, piped, and peeped, sang a few sweet notes and then made a sound like tin spoons in the gearbox of an old car. They were great mimics. Dan liked that about them, having a value for mimicry himself. He heard one imitating a nightingale, and then realized that it was a nightingale. The sedge-warbler could do a convincing nightingale (as could a starling) but not for long. All the other crazy sounds came back into his chatter. Dan stopped for a moment, pleased that his road home was being orchestrated. Then he remembered his mother's supper, and hurried on.

The moment he was indoors, he took the envelope out of his pocket and the money out of the envelope. He walked into the bright kitchen to count the money.

He stopped dead, flabbergasted. What he saw was totally unexpected. He would have said, one second before he saw it, that it was flatly impossible.

Natasha and his mother, deep in conversation, were sitting at the kitchen table. They were eating fried gammon steaks, with mashed potatoes and green peas and slices of pineapple. They had mugs of tea. They were thick as thieves, getting on like a house on fire.

Natasha looked up. There was something shocked in her face, as though she had seen a horror. She saw the money in Dan's hand, and a new expression came into her face, which was a very good face for showing expressions. Dan knew it, because he had seen it on so many faces when their owners looked at him. It was suspicion, vivid and shocking suspicion.

She thought he had killed Mrs Addison and robbed Lady Dodds-Freeman? But if she thought that, then *she* hadn't done those things.

Dan wondered which he disliked more, suspecting Natasha or being suspected by her.

'Natasha got me tea,' said Dan's mother, cheerful for the first time in months. 'She ben a sight better friend 'an ye ben a son.'

The suspicion had not left Natasha's eyes. Nor had the horror.

'They d'believe in 'at village, seemenly,' said Dan's mother, 'this maidie ben killed the poor lady. She ran away t'find ye, an' found me, an' a good job too. Who truly ben an' done it, Dan Mallett? You?'

'You?' echoed Natasha, the first word she had uttered since Dan's arrival.

'Sharron Syme saw a female wi' long fair hair, looken in the window o' the flat,' said Dan.

'What hour?' said his mother.

'Eleven.'

'Hussy prowlen the wayside at eleven? How could she see what she say she saw, a'most midnight an' folks in their beds?'

'A light in a window,' said Dan. 'Rose Winfrey's window.'

'She keepen late hours too? No good come o' that. Hours o' darkness ben for rest, else they'd aben lighten.'

This was a dig at Dan's nocturnal habits. He ignored it.

His mind gave a jolt. He said, 'Mrs Winfrey went to bed at ha'-past ten, wi' a sleepen-pill.'

'An' lef' a light a-blazen wasteful?'

'Powerful unlikely,' said Dan. 'She never lef' a light on all night before.'

'Ye seen?'

'Ben past, a time or two.'

'Wenchen or thieven,' Dan's mother told Natasha. She added, to Dan's astonishment, 'He ben a good lad at heart.'

'Then that girl made it up,' said Natasha slowly, 'about seeing somebody like me looking into the flat.'

'Rum doens,' said Dan's mother. 'Rum road t'carry on.'

'I don't believe Sharron Syme did the murder,' said Dan.

'You know her well, then?' said Natasha, staring at Dan.

'Knew her a bit, long ago,' said Dan.

He was not given to blushing, but under Natasha's scrutiny, he felt that he might be blushing.

'Either she did it, or she's protecting somebody who did it,' said Natasha. 'If not, why tell that lie?'

Dan hoped very hard it was indeed a lie. He wondered how to make sure.

'We ben obliged,' said Dan's mother, 't'find the bloke truly done it. Man or maid, make no differ. 'At way, rest o' ye ben safe.'

Dan was so surprised that he sat down hard on the third chair in the kitchen, astonishment, and the impact of his behind on the chair, causing him to bite his tongue painfully.

His mother was planning to be a detective. She was taking over the investigation, as the Yard, in detective stories, came in to control the local bluebottles.

'Find the bloke truly done it,' murmured Dan, shaking his head, his mouth full of the sharp pain of his bitten tongue.

Natasha was looking at Dan's mother with a sort of awe. Dan knew how she felt. A force of unknown power and freakish direction was being unloosed into a delicate situation. But there was no doubting that the old lady meant exactly what she said.

Dan's mother was looking at her son with tolerant contempt. She was often contemptuous of him, but rarely tolerant. It was because, he thought, she needed him for the leg-work. She would do the thinking, and he the running about. That was how she planned the unmasking of the Monk's House murderer.

'Ye see what ye best do straightaways, o' course?' said Dan's mother, with the smug air of one expecting the answer 'No'.

'Get hold of this horrible Sharron Syme, and find out who she's protecting,' said Natasha.

Dan's mother beamed – truly beamed, for the first time in years. She stretched out an arthritic claw, and patted Natasha's hand. Natasha smiled, the too-broad smile that made her look less pretty but more beautiful. Dan began to feel he was being ganged up against. He was a mere male, beset by a conspiracy of women. The whole scene remained utterly surprising.

Anyway, Natasha's answer was the right one in the view of the new boss of the murder investigation. Dan himself considered it. It was the right thing to do, but it was also impossible to do. Were they to go up to Sharron Syme, there in the hairdresser's in Milchester, and ask her who she was protecting when she invented the lie for PC Gundry? Or if, perhaps, she had done the murder herself? That scene would not play itself in Dan's mental eye. Sharron would go on lying, and she would go on being believed.

There was no way the police could know, as Dan knew, that it was highly unlikely that Rose Winfrey's bedroom light would be on at eleven o'clock. And it wasn't that Sharron had made a mistake, and named the wrong window: there was no other window whose light would show a person standing by Lady Dodds-Freeman's front door. The police would prefer Sharron's evidence to Rose Winfrey's, because Sharron was young and alert, and had been wide awake and wearing a watch, and conscious of the time because she was getting a lift back to Milchester; and Rose Winfrey was old and ill and pretty silly, and already groggy with the sleeping-pill she had taken. But Dan knew the people involved, and he thought his mother had put her funny old finger on it.

'They Medwell 'ooligans starten a yue an' cry?' Dan's mother suddenly asked Natasha.

'They were shouting about citizen's arrest,' said Natasha.

'Rum doens. Ye best bide here.'

Dan almost bit his tongue again. Never, to any living soul, had such an invitation been given. That it should be given to an unknown and very pretty girl from London was simply flabbergasting.

'Ye'll bide t'Dan's room,' said Mrs Mallett. 'Dan ben t'sleep wi' birdies or doggies.'

'I can't turn you out of your bed,' said Natasha to Dan.

It seemed to Dan that his mother winked. This was hardly more impossible than the other impossible things that had been happening; but he put it down to a trick of the dancing shadows.

Natasha, instead of Dan, put old Mrs Mallett to bed. The old lady wanted it so. Dan, who was very tired, wondered stupidly if his mother was suddenly senile. But he knew her eye was as sharp as ever, and her brain as quick. She had just taken a fancy to Natasha. It was rum.

He gave the dogs a last run, then cocooned himself in a rug in front of the kitchen range.

Natasha was, in fact, supremely safe in the cottage. Nobody would believe for a second that old Mrs Mallett would harbour a painted hussy from London. Nobody would ever look. If by some amazing chance they did, Natasha could be hiding in the Priory Woods; she was a girl who could climb out of a bedroom window and down a tree. The thing would be to get her to a telephone in the morning, to ring her cousin in the village and say she had gone to Woking or Wolverhampton. Then they could start saving their skins by finding out who had really swung the gin-bottle.

Dan found himself trying to avoid picturing that moment.

Old Mrs Mallett had been supremely satisfied by her interrogation of Natasha.

Natasha's father was a chartered accountant. The family lived in a five-bedroomed house in Surbiton, with a gravel sweep and rosebeds and a two-car garage. Natasha's father often brought work home from his City office, in a big black briefcase. He went abroad on business, taking his wife with him. The house was always very tidy, and had wall-to-wall carpeting throughout, and gas central heating. When the family was alone, they often had light suppers off an electric hostess trolley in the sitting-room.

As detail artlessly followed detail, fished out by old Mrs Mallett's cunning hand, a picture emerged which she had spent a lifetime imagining, but which she had never seen.

The respectable life.

The maid said she was trying to be an actress, but Mrs Mallett was not fooled. She was destined to be a dear little wife and mother. Mrs Mallett intended her to be Dan's wife. And once that knot was tied, the two of them would take Dan by the shoulders, and point him back in the right direction. Natasha's husband would be like Natasha's father.

Her name was really Ann. She was called Nancy at home. Natasha was her stage name – what she hoped would be a stage name. Now used to it, Mrs Mallett rather liked it, for all it sounded like a sneeze.

The old lady lay in bed, listening intently, hugging herself for her cleverness. She listened for a creak on the stairs, possibly going downwards but most likely upwards, the little villain Dan being more likely to make the running.

But she heard nothing. What was Dan thinking of, to leave the maidie alone? His father would never have missed such a chance. The old lady dropped off to sleep in a mood of exasperation; and dreamed heart-breaking dreams about Dan's father.

What was Dan thinking of? Lying in his cocoon in front of the kitchen fire, Dan was thinking about Natasha, a yard or two directly above him. He wanted her very much. But tonight was not the night, not just after she had seen a friend killed in a car-smash. She was horribly upset by that, which was what you'd expect of a girl as nice as she was. She was upset by more than her friend's death – there was more to it, but she had not said, would not say, what the 'more' was. It had to do with where she had been, the night Mrs Addison was killed. That was all Dan knew, and it was not enough.

He thought Natasha and he might come together in the end: but not if she was a murderess, and not if she thought he was a murderer. It was a proper muddle. His mother joining in might make matters easier, but Dan thought not.

Natasha, a yard or two directly above, was thinking how comforting it would be, to climb down the apple tree and creep into the kitchen. But it was impossible. Not difficult at all – perfectly easy – but impossible. Her tears wet her pillow at the thought of the mood of despair in which Laurence Catchpole had died.

And she was in appalling trouble.

And Dan was an utterly unknown quantity. He would not say where he had been on the night of the murder. He was disturbingly attractive, disarming, fascinating, difficult to disbelieve. He might easily be a thief and a murderer.

4

At breakfast (a heavy meal in the Mallett household) Dan and Natasha treated one another with cautious politeness. Old Mrs Mallett, observing them closely, saw that nothing had happened during the night, after she had gone to sleep. She was cross, not with Natasha, but with Dan. What was the good of being a devil with the girls, if you held off from the girl you really wanted?

And he wanted her, all right. There wasn't any doubt about that. When he looked at her and she wasn't looking, there couldn't be any doubt about what was going through his sneaky little mind.

Mrs Mallett was more than ever set in her purpose. She said that Natasha must stay in the cottage. She said it was the one safe place, and Natasha was welcome.

Dan had to agree that it was the safest place, but he did not understand why Natasha was welcome. Meanwhile, if Natasha were to stay, some arrangements had to be made.

After breakfast, Dan took Natasha, perilously and illegally on the pillion of his bicycle, to another village, to Medwell St Martin, where there was a public telephone outside the pub. He was known there, but there was no reason why anybody there should know Natasha.

Natasha accepted the need to find a telephone and use it, in a place where she was not known. Consequently, she accepted the need to sit on the pillion of Dan's bicycle. It meant holding him round the waist, and she accepted the need for that, or she would have fallen off, but it gave her a curious feeling.

He fascinated her. She had not the smallest idea whether to trust him or not.

She was still inclined to feel tears pricking, when she thought of the messy misery of Laurence Catchpole's death.

Dan had seen, and had said, that Natasha must use a telephone. It meant his bicycle and these little arms tight round his waist. He was disturbed and excited by this intimate physical contact which, as things were at the moment, was a peculiar element in the general mixture. He was not used to being hugged by murderesses; and while it was increasingly impossible to suspect Natasha of hitting anybody on the head with a bottle, it remained objectively possible that Sharron Syme was telling the truth, and that the person she had seen was Natasha. For if she hadn't been at the Monk's House that night, where *was* she? And if she wasn't stealing and murdering, why wouldn't she say where she was? Dan was more accustomed to being hugged by girls who thought he was a murderer, though not exactly hardened to it. If Natasha were not the murderer, then she was bound to think Dan might be, because he also wouldn't say where he had been. Dan was strongly tempted to tell Natasha the truth; but he was not ready to share with her a secret which was not his secret.

Dan sat on a gate outside Medwell St Martin, while Natasha telephoned her cousin in Medwell Fratrorum.

Her cousin Edith shrieked when she heard Natasha's voice. She already knew, from many kind friends, what had happened the previous evening – Natasha counting a lapful of money; Natasha's gentleman friend killing himself in his car, poor man; Natasha being chased through the darkness by half the village.

Natasha cut through her cousin's whimperings to communicate two vital points. The first was that she had not stolen Lady Dodds-Freeman's money or murdered Mrs Addison. The second was that she was now in Reading, well hidden, quite safe, staying with a friend, and there she would remain until the Monk's House business was sorted out. Nobody could find her, so it was no good anybody trying. Natasha thought that, though continuing to whimper, her cousin had absorbed these points. She would tell everybody, including PC Gundry, because she was a lady who told everybody everything.

No doubt the Reading police would be contacted and given her description. Natasha wished them joy of their search. Thinking this, she was surprised at herself. She had always been on the side of the police and in favour of law and order; she was not her father's daughter for nothing, even though she had graduated to a Bohemian life in Fulham. Now she was finding herself thinking of the police as ill-wishing bunglers, only less vexatious than they might have been because they were so stupid. It was a totally new way for her to think. She supposed she had absorbed some of Dan's philosophy, through her pores, from the clean cotton sheets on his bed.

Dan sat on the gate, pondering ways of carrying out the plan – his mother's plan and Natasha's. It was a good plan, the best plan, the only plan, no doubt about that; it just had the disadvantage that it was impossible.

Dan thought about the special qualities, the peculiarities of Sharron Syme. If you were making a plan involving a third party, that was what you had to do. If you made a plan to snare some pheasants, you had to know how pheasants behaved. You had to lay your angles where pheasants went, by their creepways in the dawn, from their coverts out into the fields to eat. You had to lay them so that, when the pheasants trod in them, they were caught. Then you had to have a way of dealing with the pheasants. You also had to have a way of getting away out of it without being spotted by a gamekeeper, but that was another sort of problem.

Sharron, then. Dan remembered her with gratitude and moderate goodwill. The affair had been brief, because she was a bit unvarying for his taste, and he was a bit poor for her taste. Yes, she was greedy. Cosy, obliging, good-tempered, but greedy. She was probably capable of stealing £5,000, from a rich old lady who knew where her next meal was coming from. She was certainly incapable of bashing in another old lady's skull. There were people who were capable of that and people who weren't: he hoped Natasha wasn't, and he hoped she hoped that he wasn't. About himself he was not so sure. His mother was capable of any atrocity, in defence of himself or of anyone she loved. In defence of Natasha.

Dan was sucked aside, from thoughts that mattered, into thinking about the extraordinary sudden intimacy between his mother and Natasha. It was a quirk of the old lady's for which there was no precedent and no explanation. It was clean out of character for his mother, this rapid and affectionate acceptance of a stranger.

It was not out of character for Natasha, Dan thought. She was normally an outgoing character, full of warmth and offered friendship. So perhaps Natasha could earn Sharron Syme's affection and trust, as she had earned his mother's? No. Sharron wasn't a girl's girl, never had been. She could be high on affection, but she was always low on trust. She wanted a return for affection, too, something that clinked or rustled.

Sharron's greed, that was what it kept coming back to: Sharron's eye to the main chance.

Meditating on the way to make use of Sharron's greed, Dan allowed his eyes to wander. It was a perfect mid-June morning, summer sure enough in but not yet matured to the heavy monotony of dense, deep-green foliage. Near Dan's gate there was a tall, ancient lime tree. Probably somebody had planted it – of the various sorts of lime tree, few were native – but, if so, they had stuck in the seedling a long time ago. There were small-leaved limes and large-leaved limes, and limes with in-between leaves, but at this time of year all limes seemed to have leaves of all different sizes. The leaves were of such a delicate and transparent green that the tree cast a shade different from that of any other tree, a part shade, a glowing and luminous shade. The big old tree was covered in flowers that a townsman would not have noticed, not have recognized as blossom, so far were they from the ostentatious pink and white festoons on the ornamental trees that lined their streets. Lime flowers were feathery, yellow-white, reared upwards on their supporting twigs. Millions of bees were busy among them, for these demure flowers were richer in nectar than anything else in the countryside, at this season. Lime was the key honey-flow, this tide, for bee-keepers hereabouts. Dan, whose finicky mother liked a drop of young lime honey, was grateful to the bees and the limes and their unobtrusive, nectar-dripping flowers.

He forced his mind back to business. Sharron, now. Her greed, now.

In the topmost branches of the lime two birds were singing, a blackbird and a throstle. Cousins, but quite different; it was most unusual to see the two of them singing side by side and quite ignoring one another.

Lime, blossom, honey, bees, blackbird, thrush. Suddenly Dan saw a way of finding out what Sharron Syme was at.

Twirlies, Ladies' and Gentlemen's hairdresser, East Street, Milchester, was a superior establishment, dominated by the charismatic personality of Mr Adrian. All the girls would have loved him, except that there was evidently no percentage in doing so. It was refined work, and a lovely way to meet people. If a girl gave a gentleman a shampoo, before Mr Adrian gave him his haircut and blow-wave (he always preferred cutting wet, ladies and gentlemen both, in the modern way), she could get to know him ever so easily. Sharron Syme liked getting to know gentlemen easily. She could judge them, when their heads were over the basin: state of their collars, state of their necks and ears, standard of their jolly remarks. They mostly made jolly remarks, as not many of them had got quite used to having their hair shampooed by a girl. You could lean against them a bit, if you liked them; it was wonderful how many gin-and-oranges came of that.

More besides, if you knew a bit about them.

There were a common pub and a genteel pub in the same street as the salon. Sharron always met her new friends, and her old friends, in the saloon bar of the genteel pub. What she did afterwards depended on a lot of things.

The police interrogated Dan Mallett, the afternoon of Natasha's call to her cousin. He was almost incoherently rural; he had not seen hair or hide of that Lunnon maid, who, he understood in the village, had bashed old Mrs Addison on the head wi' a bottle.

They came to search the cottage, sufficiently advertising their arrival. They poked about in Dan's little bedroom, while Dan stood grinning oafishly, twisting his cap in his hands. Old Mrs Mallett seemed to be stone-deaf; it had come on in recent weeks, seemingly; her teeth clashed in senile fury.

Natasha was deep in the hazel-clumps of the Priory Woods, until Dan's whistle recalled her. Their reunion was, as at breakfast, cautiously polite.

She looked so sweet, coming dishevelled out of the undergrowth, that Dan was once again tempted to drop all caution, and either drop politeness too, or be much more polite, depending how you looked at it; he was tempted to grab her and kiss her and hope for the best.

But he had to give her more time, after the horror of the previous evening. And he had to know more about her.

He had to know what happened on the night of the murder.

Dan bicycled into Milchester, a weary way. In the town, without his bicycle, he became invisible – just a little browny nothing among the parked cars. He flitted up and down East Street, taking in Twirlies and the two pubs. At 5.45 he watched Sharron, out of her nylon overall and into a figure-hugging sweater, tittup down the street from Twirlies. She passed Ward's the department store, where, in the dreadful days of his slavery, Dan had bought shirts with semi-stiff collars. Behind one of the plate-glass windows of Ward's there were half a dozen figures not closely resembling men, very tanned, with hair like young Mr Guy Heron's, wearing clothes for beach, poolside and tennis court; behind the next window stood ladies with hair like Natasha's, in shifts and caftans. All the dummies looked as though, if alive, they would have patronized the more horrible of the two pubs in East Street. The end of the ladies' window was boarded up; a sign apologized for any inconvenience to customers.

Sharron went past the windows, and into the horrible pub, the one with blond wood and fairy lights. It was the pub Dan had picked for her to go into. She was joined by the companion he had, more or less, picked for her to be joined by – a man who looked as though he bought vodka and bitter lemon for the girls he met on his travels, and charged them to his expense account.

Next morning was Dan's morning at Lady Dodds-Freeman's. He turned up punctually, bobbed, grinned, tugged his forelock, and accepted a cup of coffee. He followed her into the flat. There was no sign of horrible violence: the blood had been scrubbed away and everything knocked over replaced. The flat looked odd, denuded, without all the Georgian silver. Lady Dodds-Freeman sat down in the kitchen, and began talking, semi-coherently, about an insult offered her, forty years previously, on Sandown racecourse. Dan clucked sympathetically, and, clucking, crept out of the kitchen. He went to the extension telephone in the bedroom, and called Twirlies in Milchester.

He asked for Sharron Syme. He admitted it was private business, but urgent.

'Helloo,' said Sharron's voice, as refined as could be: you could imagine her undulating slightly as she said it.

Dan adopted the tones of a man who might have offered a lady an insult on Sandown racecourse, forty years before. 'Jack Maltravers, Captain,*' he said. 'Remember me?'

'Ooh Captain,' said Sharron, 'I'm sure I will when I see you.'

'Lathered my nob a few weeks ago,' said Dan, keeping an eye on the door in case Lady Dodds-Freeman had an access of sanity, and came to see who was imitating captains in her bedroom. 'When I offered you a snifter, you took a raincheck. Well, the bad penny's turned up. Made a few bob at Sandown the other day, want to celebrate with a beaker or two in congenial company. I can't think of any company more congenial than yours, my dear, so how's about this evening when you leave the old snippery?'

Dan was aware that, in adopting the air of a raffish Captain, he was overplaying the part as grossly as he overplayed his antique yokel. He did not think Sharron would mind.

Sharron did not mind. She was agreeable to meeting Captain Maltravers, and all the money he had won at Sandown, in the pub with the fairy lights in East Street.

'You'll probably recognize me,' said Dan. 'I'm the one you

* The scarcely credible reasons for Dan's choice of this pseudonym will be found in *Bait on the Hook*, by the same author.

said reminded you of Thingummy, the actor. Sure as eggs is eggs I'll recognize you.'

The necessity of talking in this ridiculous way caused Dan to contort his face into that of a man wearing an ill-fitting monocle. He hung up to find Lady Dodds-Freeman in the doorway, staring at him with eyes that might not be entirely glazed. He scuttled out of the room, grinning and bobbing, and bolted into the garden.

They now needed a car.

Dan had, potentially, the keys of several local cars, but the vehicles were more comfortably available in the middle of the night – when, indeed, Dan more usually wanted them – than in the middle of the day.

After lunch, prepared with cheerful bangings by Natasha, Dan went off on his bicycle. He pedalled with carefullest casualness past the Potters at the Mill, past Dr Smith and Admiral Jenkyn, seeing either the owners of the cars in their gardens, or empty garages with open doors. In the end he had to stoop to Fred Dawson's Ford pick-up, which had no seats in the back. He hid his bicycle, and drove the pick-up to his cottage.

After tea (what Natasha called tea, at four-thirty, not what Mrs Mallett called tea) Natasha helped Mrs Mallett into the passenger's seat of the van. It was Natasha's help Mrs Mallett wanted, not Dan's. Natasha scrambled into the back, which she had to share with Fred Dawson's rotary mower, and Dan drove to Milchester. Mrs Mallett wore a black straw hat and her Sunday coat which reeked of mothballs; Dan thought the last time she had worn these garments was at his father's funeral. She endowed the expedition with massive respectability; nobody would have guessed – would have dared guess – that the van was borrowed without the owner's knowledge or consent, and that it contained two fugitive murder suspects, to see the prim, tight-lipped old lady sitting beside the driver.

Dan parked in East Street. On Natasha's arm, Mrs Mallett hobbled to the Plough just after it opened. Inside, the Plough was all that Dan had guessed from its outside – soft piped music, pink tables and patterned wallpaper. Mrs Mallett looked round in astonished admiration; it was the kind of interior she yearned for; it put her in mind of the kind of house that had a two-toned doorbell.

Dan and Natasha installed the old lady on a pink chair at one of the pink tables. She had her back to the party wall which divided the saloon bar from the public; leaning against the arm of her chair was her rubber-tipped stick. From where she sat she could see the whole bar and, through the glass in a swing door, the public telephone. Dan bought her a glass of port. Sitting in a corner of the saloon bar, behind her glass of port, in her black straw hat, she faded at once into the background: most pubs in English country towns contain one or more inconspicuous old ladies drinking port by themselves.

Natasha and Dan left Mrs Mallett: dissociated themselves from her completely. Dan bought whisky for himself and vodka and tonic for Natasha, with Major Coxen's money. They sat on stools at the far end of the bar, in a place from which they could see the door to the street.

Sharron Syme came in, plump and very clean, wearing a different but equally tight cotton sweater. She perched on a stool, looking happy to be meeting Captain Maltravers and his Sandown winnings. She gossiped softly with the barmaid, keeping an eye on the door. The pub was still almost empty.

Leaving Natasha, Dan went down the bar and offered Sharron a drink. He used the banker's voice which had always been the voice for Sharron. She gave a mannered shriek, and accepted a gin and bitter lemon. She still kept an eye on the door.

'Should you be drinking gin, so soon after concussion?' said Dan.

'Ooh yes, Ai'm fully recovered, thanks ever so much,' said Sharron.

Dan asked her about the girl she had seen at the window of Lady Dodds-Freeman's flat at eleven o'clock on the night of the murder. Sharron was happy to talk about it: too happy. Providing important evidence in a murder investigation had made her into a kind of celebrity, even though, Dan thought, the evidence was a lie. Probably she had told the story so many times she almost believed it.

The barmaid moved away, not to serve another customer

but, Dan thought, because she had heard the story so often she was sick of it.

Very gently and cajolingly, Dan suggested to Sharron that she might have been mistaken. He did not think he was as good at being cajoling in his banker's voice as in his treacly rural voice, but he did his best.

It was no good. Sharron stuck firmly by her story. She was word-perfect in it.

Dan beckoned to Natasha, who joined them. She and Sharron looked at one another without recognition; their paths might have crossed in Medwell Fratrorum, but had evidently not done so.

'Was this the girl you saw?' asked Dan.

A brief mental struggle showed in Sharron's face. It would be highly convenient for her – and for whomever she was protecting, Dan guessed – to identify Natasha. It would also be incredible, and Sharron was quite clever enough to see that.

'I was quite a way away,' said Sharron, with evident regret. 'I only saw the back. There wasn't much light.'

'There wasn't any light,' said Natasha. 'Are you lying to protect yourself or somebody else?'

Sharron appeared greatly shocked. She was not accustomed to having her word doubted. She had gone to the police with her story, because it was her duty and the story was the truth.

'Would five hundred quid change your mind?' asked Dan.

Sharron stared at him, her mouth dropping open. She did not immediately say 'No'. She took a sip of her drink, to cover her visible indecision and to give herself time to think.

She said, 'You haven't got five hundred pounds. You never did have.'

'I have,' said Natasha, in a tone compelling belief. Even Dan, who knew it was untrue, believed Natasha for a moment.

'You don't have to say you were fibbing,' said Dan. 'You don't have to say there wasn't anybody there, or there wasn't any light, or you were nowhere near the place. Just that you've thought and thought about it, as your duty was, and now you're a lot less certain. People will think better of you, really. Myself, I'd like people to think better of me. I'd like five hundred quid, too.'

Sharron was not one for turning down five hundred pounds out of hand, especially, Dan concluded, for telling the truth instead of a lie which might still blow up in her face. There was no longer any doubt in Dan's mind that it was a lie: Sharron's hesitation ended all possibility of that.

'It would have to be a lot more than five hundred,' said Sharron finally.

The remark fitted with everything Dan knew about her.

'How much more?' asked Natasha, as though price was no problem.

'I'll have to let you know later,' said Sharron. 'Later this evening or tomorrow.'

Dan understood. This was a Dutch auction. Sharron was selling her evidence to the highest bidder.

'I'll meet you here at ten,' said Sharron.

'I can't get any money this evening,' said Natasha.

'No, but if you've really got it, you can have it by dinnertime tomorrow.'

Dan wondered if 'dinnertime' to Sharron meant midday or evening. It depended on how intelligently she had been doing her social climbing. The point was without importance, because Natasha was never going to give her any money.

'You must go now,' said Sharron.

Yes, so that they would not see her friend, the other bidder in the auction.

'Right,' said Dan. 'But don't wait for Captain Maltravers. He doesn't exist.'

'You tricked me!' said Sharron, an angry hairdresser.

'A mite, but the way it's turning out we're doing you a good turn.'

'I can't promise anything,' said Sharron.

No, not until she had received the other bid.

Dan and Natasha left the pub. They did not look in old Mrs Mallett's direction. They went straight to Fred Dawson's van. Dan used the wing-mirror of a parked car to observe the door of the pub. As he expected, Sharron appeared in the door. She was watching them into the van and away. They got into the van, and went away.

Dan drove round a corner, and parked out of sight of the

Plough. They went back to the pub, but into the public bar. The atmosphere and decor were quite different, and much better, though the piped music was still audible over the crash of a fruit-machine. They were invisible to anybody in the saloon bar, and their voices inaudible.

Dan bought drinks.

They were able, after a few minutes, to edge their way to the corner, to a place against the wall. The saloon bar was the other side of the wall; Dan's mother was just the other side of the wall from where they stood.

Old Mrs Mallett watched the conversation at the bar with close attention. She deplored her dainty little Natasha getting involved with riffraff like that Sharron Syme, but she knew it was necessary; it was Natasha's own plan, and her future mother-in-law's. It was lucky for Dan, having the two of them to tell him what to do.

Dan and Natasha left, and immediately, as they had expected, Sharron went through the swing door to the telephone.

Dan and Natasha would not be in position, yet, on the other side of the wall, so there was no point in communicating news about the telephone.

Sharron came back from the telephone. She smoked a cigarette. Old Mrs Mallett had never smoked, and disapproved of women doing so in public. Her little Natasha did not smoke. She said it was because she had trained to be a singer, as well as all the other things, but really it was because she was too dainty to indulge in such a messy habit, and too economical to indulge in such an extravagant one.

Sharron was nursing the drink Dan had foolishly bought her. She was waiting for her friend, the one she had summoned by telephone; he would buy her next drink. She was too mean to buy one for herself. There was a difference between good sense and meanness.

Sharron's friend arrived. He was in his fifties, maybe nearing sixty. It was shocking to see the furtive intimacy with which he and Sharron greeted one another. There was no doubting their relationship, Mrs Mallett thought. He wore sporty tweeds with a loud check, and a very hairy felt hat. Mrs Mallett had never seen him, but he was one of a type she had seen all too often. He was the sort who pretended to be a countryman instead of staying sensibly in the suburbs like Natasha's father.

Mrs Mallett knocked on the wall behind her with the handle of her walking stick. She made it look like something she did by mistake. There was an answering knock, inaudible in the saloon bar to anybody except her. Dan's knuckles, or an ashtray.

Sharron's friend bought her a drink, since she had quickly finished off Dan's drink the moment the newcomer arrived. She was that sort of girl.

They were having a fierce old discussion, the two of them. During the course of it, the tweedy man handed Sharron something, an envelope. That didn't end the discussion. It was all exactly as Mrs Mallett and Natasha had expected – Sharron was being paid but she wanted more.

The man finished his drink and put on his hat. Before going he bought Sharron another drink. They weren't going to leave together, to be seen together in the street.

Mrs Mallett knocked on the wall behind her with her stick. She listened for the acknowledging knock, and heard it. Dan would be out of the public bar and hiding somewhere, before the other man left the saloon bar.

Dan stood in the doorway of a shop, trying to work a cigarette-lighter which was, in fact, the key of Fred Dawson's van.

He expected the man who came out of the pub to be well known to him by sight, and to know him well by sight.

Aidan Winfrey came out of the pub.

But surely he was in London?

He wasn't in London, and never had been. He'd been down here throughout, in or near Milchester, shacked up with Sharron Syme, a few minutes in a car from Medwell and the Monk's House.

If he was offering Sharron money, it certainly wasn't his money, because he didn't have any.

Supremely obviously, then, it was Lady Dodds-Freeman's money.

5

'But his wife rang him up in London,' said Natasha.

'His wife said she spoke to him on the telephone,' said Dan.

'Oh. If he started the call he might have been anywhere. He might have been in this pub.'

'Likely. It's where he and Sharron meet. His wife told him about Lady Dodds-Freeman's silver, and money like fallen leaves all over that flat. He needed money, because Sharron always wants money.'

'Sharron could have given him an alibi. Sold him an alibi.'

'Yes, and you say somebody could give you an alibi, and I know somebody could give me an alibi, but it's not a bit of use to any of us. Rose Winfrey's horribly possessive, and being an invalid makes it worse.'

'Oh. If she thought she was buying his ticket to London, and really she was buying drinks for Sharron . . .'

'The balloon'd go up in that family. No more rounds in the Chestnut Horse, no more subscription to the golf club, no more Sharron.'

'Why couldn't he go out and make some money?' said Natasha. 'He's not that old.'

'That's Surbiton speaking,' said Dan. 'There's people who never can make any money. But they want it just as bad as people who can make it.'

'So they murder for it?'

'Seems he did. I wonder how we can prove it?'

A knock on the wall behind them told them that Sharron had left the pub. They went round to the saloon bar, and Dan helped his mother to her feet.

'Sharron never spotted you?' he said.

'Nay. Who'd look at an old 'oman setten wi' a small port?'

'What do we do now?' asked Natasha.

'You an' me bes' put our thinken-caps on, dearie, an' calc'late a road for t' trap un.'

'That would be best,' said Dan meekly.

Dan delivered his mother and her new favourite at the cottage. He did not quite deliver the van to Fred Dawson, though he felt bad about not doing so. The whole thing had taken longer than he had expected, and Fred would be home, and telephoning to PC Gundry, and it would all be thoroughly unsympathetic. Dan parked the van where he could wriggle out of it unobserved. Before doing so, he wiped the steering-wheel and ignition-key with his handkerchief. He did not think the police would fingerprint a van, though borrowed unbeknownst, which had been returned almost to its owner's door, but it was best to play safe. He wanted no more black marks chalked up against his name, this tide. He pulled his bicycle out of its hiding-place, and pedalled slowly home through the soft evening.

It was almost dark. Dog-daisies winked like stars in the verges, and beyond the hedges the hay was nearly all cut. The bicycle went tick-tick-tick, and the tyres whispered on the tarmac. Over these faint, familiar sounds, Dan heard the deep coo of a turtle-dove, and then the ugly, nasal complaint of one of those collared doves which had suddenly become so common, having been unheard of in those parts a few years previously.

They were going to set a trap for Aidan Winfrey; just so; and his mother and Natasha were going to make a plan. He thought he had better suggest a plan to his mother, and then make her think it was all her idea. The trouble was, he had no plan. Aidan Winfrey must have some way of convincing people he really had been in London . . . perhaps another bought alibi, or perhaps he had been there just for an hour or two. If it came to his word against Dan's, it would be like Major Coxen all over again. Winfrey would be sensible about the stolen money; he wouldn't throw it about, except quietly to Sharron. If he and Sharron stood firm, it was going to be very hard to pin anything on either of them. As far as Dan could see, it was going to be impossible, although it was entirely necessary.

Dan got home to find Natasha cooking supper and his mother drinking stout. It was a most agreeable domestic scene. Dan was astonished all over again; the stiff whisky he poured himself had a flavour of astonishment.

'We were supposed to be meeting that horrible girl again, at ten o'clock,' said Natasha,

'Gum, so we were,' said Dan. 'Shock of seeing Winfrey put it out of my mind. So be, she'll have to buy her own drinks.'

'I doubt it.'

'Hussy a-smoken,' said Dan's mother.

'If he'd met Sharron in that pub on the night of the murder,' said Natasha suddenly, 'people would have seen him. Anywhere public, people would have seen him. That barmaid, or some other barmaid, or somebody. And early in the evening he hadn't murdered anybody, so he didn't really need to pretend to be in London, except to his wife. So we ought to be able to prove he was down here.'

'Not so easy,' said Dan. 'First off, he was likely holed up in a motel with Sharron, "Mr and Mrs Smith", ever so discreet. Second, we're not like the bluebottles. We can't commandeer a recent photograph, an' traipse all over Milchester saying, "Did you see this bloke on Monday night?" Third, proving he was hereabouts is a right long road from proving he did a robbery and a murder.'

'A motel,' murmured Natasha. She blushed at the memory of her own innocent night; she shuddered at the memory of Laurence's violent death.

'They motels ben sinks of iniquity,' said Mrs Mallett, who had read about rum doings in the local paper.

Natasha served up the supper. Mrs Mallett waxed lyrical about it; she compared Natasha's dainty cooking very favourably with Dan's. It was not clear to Dan if this was partly genuine praise of Natasha, or wholly a dig at Dan. Whatever she said, she ate no more than usual.

After supper, Natasha was not allowed to help Dan with the washing-up. She had done enough. She was to sit by Mrs Mallett, and they were to put their thinking-caps on.

Dan watched them, amused and deeply thankful. They made a plan. It was that Aidan Winfrey should be trapped into confessing, or otherwise revealing, his guilt of murder and robbery, this revelation to be in a form which would convince the police. That was the plan; the details of method were humdrum, and could be left to Dan.

Once again, it was Natasha who put Dan's mother to bed.

Once again, old Mrs Mallett lay listening for creaks on the stairs and jangles of bedsprings; and, not hearing anything, went to sleep mentally abusing Dan for not being more wicked than he was.

Dan was now certain that Natasha had not committed any crime, and could not commit any violent crime. Since they knew Aidan Winfrey had murdered Mrs Addison while stealing the £5,000, Dan now knew Natasha hadn't, and she knew he hadn't.

But what *had* she been doing instead, which she still wouldn't tell him about?

And why couldn't she accept his word, that he had been up to no harm that night?

And how long did it take a girl to get over seeing somebody killed in a car smash?

In the morning Dan bicycled round to the Monk's House. It was not his day to go there, but it was reasonable that, after the tragedy, he should look in to see if he was needed.

He was not needed in the least. PC Gundry was there, drinking a cup of coffee; Lady Dodds-Freeman was drinking white wine. PC Gundry was trying to jog the old lady's memory about the night of the murder: about whether she had locked the door or unlocked the door, where she had put the money, what she had seen or heard. It was no good. She had been in a drunken stupor.

Dan saw Aidan Winfrey. He had come home the previous evening, therefore he had been quite safe letting himself be seen in Milchester. Had he not been going home that evening, obviously he would have met Sharron Syme somewhere secret. That explained one of the puzzles.

He was working in his part of the garden, building a rustic pergola. He was dressed in ancient corduroys and a tweed deer-stalker hat. He was dressed up as a country gentleman building a pergola; he had overdressed for the part, in that ridiculous hat; he was trying too hard. He was exaggerating as grossly as Dan exaggerated his yokel role or his Captain Maltravers role.

Dan pondered Aidan Winfrey, as he had pondered Sharron Syme. Her simple greed had made her easy to trick. This was a more complicated problem. Aidan Winfrey liked golf. He liked showing off. He hid his failure and inadequacy, his humiliating dependence on his wife, behind all that hearty bluster. He was greedy enough to steal £5,000; he had not murdered for it, but in order not to be caught stealing it. So what? Dan saw no clear path through any of this.

Young Mr Guy Heron, home to support his mother in her bereavement, got tired of supporting her after a bit, and went off in his sports-car. He was wearing a black tie, but the car struck a frivolous note.

Shortly afterwards Mrs Heron came out of her flat, in a sort of piebald half-mourning. She called to Mr Winfrey, something about a stuck cupboard-door. Hearty and neighbourly as always, he immediately abandoned his pergola, picked up his tools, and followed her indoors. He was doing something free, thought Dan sourly, which in the proper order of things Dan would be doing for money. Young Mr Guy Heron, perhaps, was not good at fixing doors, or had more important things on his mind. Mr Winfrey seemed not very good at it, either; anyway he was a very long time about it.

Dan gave Aidan Winfrey up. He bicycled slowly home, stopping in the village to shop at the post office. He was treated warily. A lot of people were amazed he was not behind bars. He was a little amazed at this himself. If they found Natasha, she'd be behind bars in no time.

He got home to find they were doing some late spring cleaning; there were millions of motes of dust in the sunbeams that filtered through the overarching trees into the windows of the cottage.

'Natasha ben scrubben,' said Dan's mother. 'A-did try t'stop un, but she'm wilful.' There was pride and even love in her voice.

'There was practically nothing to do,' said Natasha. 'You've kept the place beautifully clean.'

'Gammon,' said Mrs Mallet. 'T'were kin to a pigsty.'

Dan told them Aidan Winfrey was home, and that he had therefore been perfectly safe in showing his face in the saloon bar of the Plough.

'But there's a lot they don't know we know,' said Natasha. 'We know he wasn't in London but somewhere nearby, because he was there a few minutes after Sharron called. And she knew he was there. They don't know we know that. Anybody else in the pub might have thought he'd just got off the London train, but we know better, and they don't know we know. Or that they're friends. Or that he gave her what must have been money. We know she's lying about the light in Rose Winfrey's window, even though nobody else would think that was a lie. We know he's got plenty of money which he couldn't have come by honestly.'

'Do we *know* that, exactly?' said Dan.

'Yes, of course. Sharron wouldn't bother with him for long, if he didn't have plenty of money.'

'We know a sight of things,' said Dan. 'Knowledge is power,' he added vaguely, remembering being told this, years before at school, to persuade him to diligence with his books.

He turned suddenly to Natasha, and said, 'Can you do Sharron Syme?'

'Ooh,' said Natasha, painfully refined. 'It's ever so kaind of you to ask.'

'Lovely. Overdoing it a mite, I think.'

'But,' said Natasha in her ordinary voice, which was not quite like an ordinary person's ordinary voice, 'I don't know what she'd say.'

'Unless she's changed, and I don't think she has, I know exactly what she'd say. I'll be your script-writer.'

'Is she going to talk to Aidan Winfrey?'

'Yes, of course.'

'Probably they have pet-names. Sort of a private language. I mean, for instance, d'you suppose she calls him "darling"?'

'The idea,' said Dan's mother.

'Hum,' said Dan. 'Not at a moment of crisis. Not on the telephone. At least, I don't think so. He'd be more a one for pet-names, I'd guess. She's on the phone, she's rattled, she's in a hurry, she's got to meet him. I think she'd say "Hello", and get on with it. Specially if money's involved.'

'Schemen hussy,' said Dan's mother.

'I need ever so much, ever so urgently,' said Natasha in Sharron's voice. In her own voice she said, 'Why do I need it?'

'Fur coat in the sales?' suggested Dan.

'She makes a date with him, and we keep it,' said Natasha. 'But suppose he has a think and rings her back? Then they know somebody's after them. And, if she knows you as well as I think she does, she might guess it was you.'

'Cloven hoof,' said Dan's mother. 'Any mischief yereabouts, 'tes commonly Dan.'

'He can't ring her back,' said Dan. 'She's left the phone. She's already on her way to meet him. She's told him so.'

'Hum,' said Natasha, having picked up this useful word from Dan. 'Suppose he won't come?'

'Then we'll think of something else.'

'Conversations don't always go the way you plan them.'

'This one won't have a chance of going any other way. More of a monologue. "Pick up your feet an' belt round to see me, or else."'

'She wouldn't say that, would she?'

'No. Something like, "Honestly you must dash round, it's really ever so urgent."'

"Honestly you must dash round,' said Natasha in Sharron's voice, 'I'm reelly ever so anxious.'

'Ben magical,' said Dan's mother. 'Ben a differ maid talken.'

'So we get him into a trap,' said Natasha. 'Then what do we do?'

'We blackmail him,' said Dan. 'We know he killed one old lady, an' stole another old lady's money. We saw him.'

'What does he do?'

'He either pays us, or he promises to pay us, or he tries to kill us. Any of those three, he's admitting guilt.'

'Suppose he calls our bluff?'

'What bluff? We do know he did it. How else did he come by enough money to buy not only Sharron but her evidence too?'

'Well, it's bluff that we saw him.'

'I don't think he'll call it. He's murdered once to stay out of trouble. I imagine the first one is the hardest. Gets to be easier after a bit, like anything else. Gets to be a habit.'

'The idea,' said Dan's mother.

Dan rehearsed Natasha in the locutions of Sharron Syme, and Natasha rehearsed herself in Sharron's voice. She tended to slip into exaggeration, as Dan himself did with various voices, and as Aidan Winfrey did with his country clothes. Dan thought it was a fault on the right side: Aidan Winfrey would not be sensitive to the nuances of refined-shopgirl speech. And almost certainly Sharron slightly caricatured herself on the telephone, as most people did. And anyway Natasha was a professional, and would end up more like Sharron Syme than Sharron Syme was.

Dan was morally sure, by lunch time, that they could get Aidan Winfrey to meet them in a private place, with either money in his pocket or a shotgun in his hands.

The coroner held his preliminary inquest, that afternoon, in the Milchester police station. Mrs Heron testified to the identity of her sister's body, and the pathologist as to the cause of death. The Detective Chief-Superintendent reassured the coroner that enquiries were being pursued, and an arrest was expected shortly. The coroner adjourned the proceedings.

The regulars at the Chestnut Horse heard all about it. It was Natasha's arrest that was expected shortly.

Natasha herself, by day, was beginning to look extremely odd. Of her own clothes, she had only those in which she had run away from the village. There was no way she could retrieve other clothes from her cousin's house, and Dan could not collect anything for her without revealing that he was in contact with Natasha.

Consequently, when her own clothes were unsuitable, or

were being washed, she wore things of Dan's and things of his mother's. Dan's clothes were becoming but did not fit; his mother's clothes fitted but were not becoming. It was not important. If she went out by daylight, it was straight into the tangled depths of the Priory Woods. Nobody saw her, or was to be allowed to see her.

When they went out late in the afternoon to telephone, they went on foot, though it was a long way to walk. The pillion of Dan's bicycle was no place for Natasha to be. Since she was going to be invisible, she could wear clothes chosen without regard to appearance. From the waist up she resembled someone in a schoolgirl production of *Gammer Gurton's Nedle*, and from the waist down she resembled Charlie Chaplin in *Modern Times*.

No public telephone was safe. Milchester would probably have been safe, owing to the crowds, but Milchester was too far to walk, and Dan did not feel like crowding his luck by borrowing another car. In all the villages, the public telephones were glass boxes in front of post offices; going into one was like going on to a stage or a film-set.

What they wanted was an empty house. It had to be a house, rather than a cottage. Cottages were always more difficult to get into, owing to the suspicious natures of cottage people; and they were apt to be close together, under continual observation from one another owing to women checking up on one anothers' morals and expenditure. Isolated cottages were not on the telephone, unless they belonged to farm managers or gamekeepers, and people like that were never away; even when they went out, they were apt to pop back in, to create an embarrassing predicament for anybody borrowing the telephone.

Dan made it his business to know which nobs were away. He also knew which ones installed house-sitters, to keep the place warm and look after the dogs and discourage burglars and borrowers of telephones. Sir George and Lady Simpson were away, but they had imported a retired schoolmaster and his wife, at crippling cost, to keep the garden in order, and to keep Dan in order when he worked in the garden. Doctor Smith was away, fishing in Ireland, but he had a fancy telephone with an answering machine, which gave callers the numbers of other doctors. Dan thought he could disconnect the recording, but he was not sure he could reconnect it, and he did not want people to be unable to get a doctor.

The answer, inconveniently far away, was a much-restored house called Woodbines. Mr and Mrs Calloway were in Greece. They had nothing much of value. (They had had some moderate silver, but Dan had decided that his need for money for his mother's operation was greater than their need for tureens and soup-spoons. Mr Calloway had been, on balance, pleased; he had grossly overclaimed on his insurance, as Dan knew from his delicious daughter-in-law.)

Dan and Natasha walked to Woodbines, by Dan's route for walking to Woodbines, which was not the route anybody else would have chosen; it had the merit of invisibility, but it involved the use of holes through hedges, so it was fortunate that Natasha was dressed, in part, for going through holes in hedges.

Peewits were all over the fields, in flocks again after going off in private pairs to breed. Their crests stuck up as bravely as in the spring, but they seemed morose and apathetic. They were not in the mood for their marvellous aerobatic flying, on great round-ended wings, or for the haunting call their name imitated. They would be idle and dispirited until the autumn rains softened the ground; then they would dig about for insects under the surface, and in their glee at getting better dinners, form tumbling and soaring squadrons, and cry to each other about going south.

The other most noticeable companions of their journey were orange-tip butterflies, which Natasha, to Dan's amazement, had never seen before. He understood that they would not have thrived in the streets of Chelsea and Fulham, but he thought they would have been happy in a garden in Surbiton. Perhaps they were, and she had simply never looked. What they liked were the various sorts of mustard, like charlock and wild radish and pepperwort, all in flower in June, all yellow and a bit dull and glamourless, and common in the verges and on the edges of arable fields. The orange-tips were sly. They laid their eggs on the stems of these plants; then the caterpillars looked like the long seed-pods of all those mustardy plants; and then the chrysalises looked like dead leaves. Dan showed them all to Natasha. She was fascinated by the contrast between the camouflaged obscurity of the earlier stages, and the brilliant ostentation of the adult.

'Bit like yourself,' said Dan. 'Hiding in disguise one tide, an' stepping out into the spotlight the next.'

'I'm beginning to wonder if that will ever happen.'

'Shame. Must have faith in yourself.'

'Hum. I've got stage-fright now, about this performance of Sharron.'

'Sounded good to me. D'you want to run through it again?'

'No. It's a mistake to over-rehearse. How do you know so much about birds and bugs and flowers?'

'Living amongst them. My Dad taught me a lot, but a lot of what he taught me he learned from his Dad, and a lot of it's not quite right. I don't make a study of caterpillars. But if they're there I see them.'

'So do I, now. Look, these are caterpillars.'

'Those,' said Dan, 'are seed-pods.'

'Well, they're imitating caterpillars, for protection against caterpillars.'

'I wonder if you've made a discovery,' said Dan. 'I suppose those dead leaves are imitating chrysalises so as not to be eaten by a cow.'

'Will Aidan Winfrey really try to kill us?'

'Hard to predict. Be interesting to see.'

They reached Woodbines a little after six. Dan prowled round the over-dainty house, and confirmed that it was empty. No burglar-alarm had been installed.

Dan went to the garden shed, where he had once kissed the Calloways' daughter-in-law. Behind a loose brick he found the front-door keys, Yale and Chubb, which Mr Calloway thought he had lost while making a bonfire. They went in, like Christians, through the front door, which Dan locked behind them.

'Time for a drink,' said Dan. 'But don't touch anything you can't wipe clean.'

'You sound like a professional criminal.'

'No, pretty amateur . . .'

There was a telephone in the drawing-room with an extension

in the kitchen and another upstairs. They looked up the Winfreys' number in the local directory; Natasha dialled it while Dan listened on the kitchen extension.

Mrs Winfrey answered, the invalid Rose who'd unknowingly bought some of Sharron's drinks until Lady Dodds-Freeman had the privilege.

Aidan Winfrey was at the Milchester Golf Club.

The office put the call through to the bar. There was a buzz of conversation and a muffled burst of laughter when the barman picked up his telephone. He called for Mr Winfrey. So far, Natasha had used her normal voice.

'Winfrey,' said Aidan Winfrey, as though he was a man used to wheeling and dealing on the telephone.

'Helloo,' said Natasha in Sharron's voice, moderately overdoing it. 'Something ever so strange has happened, I must talk to you.'

'Talk.'

'Noo, not now, I've only got a sec, Gloria's just coming in.'

Gloria was the name of Dan's tamest and greediest blue-marble bantam hen; they had agreed that it was a name a friend of Sharron's would have.

'Where are you?' said Aidan Winfrey.

To Dan, listening in the kitchen, it appeared that Aidan Winfrey thought Natasha was Sharron. He would almost have thought so himself.

'In the village. This is Gloria's phone.'

'Who the hell's Gloria?'

'She's may friend, isn't she? When are you coming hoome?'

'Any minute, but Christ, you can't turn up there.'

'Ooh, noo, but we could meet somewhere.'

Something in Natasha's Sharron voice alerted Aidan Winfrey. And of course he knew Sharron.

'This sounds to me like money,' he said.

'Yes. Ay'm ever so sorry, but Ay do need some. Not for mayself. Ooh, Gloria's coming. Noo, you can't phone back, I have to go out to meet someone, to promise them five hundred pounds.'

'Jesus Christ.'

'There's much worse things can happen than parting with five hundred pounds.'

'Hmm.' Aidan Winfrey sounded as though nothing much worse could happen than giving Sharron another gigantic bribe. Then, it seemed to Dan, he reflected that very much worse things could happen. He said he would meet Sharron at 10.30 in the usual place.

As Natasha had no idea what their usual place was, she said no, not the usual place for ever so many reasons, but the summerhouse at the bottom of the garden at the Monk's House.

Aidan Winfrey made puzzled noises, by which Dan and Natasha realized that the summerhouse *was* their usual place. This calamitous coincidence threatened to be disastrous.

'Ooh, silly me, I'm that rattled, I was thinking of Milchester,' said Natasha, in a rattled voice which represented serious overacting. Not being able to stand any more of this, she added, 'Ooh, now Gloria reelly is coming in, so bye-bye for now and Abyssinia.'

They had rehearsed 'Abyssinia'; Natasha had objected to it, on the grounds that it was too old-fashioned for Sharron, but Dan assured her Sharron did say it, or had (he cleared his throat, embarrassed) at one time.

'See you later, alligator,' said Aidan Winfrey, almost equally old-fashioned.

They set off after Natasha had put Dan's mother to bed. For once – for the very first time – Dan's mother was neither angry nor suspicious about a late-night expedition. Natasha was involved; she would keep Dan out of trouble. Also they were trying to carry out her plan and Natasha's, of trapping that Aidan Winfrey. Left on his own, Dan would probably make a mess of it. Even with Natasha, the two of them might easily make a mess of it, because Natasha, though well-meaning as well as sweetly pretty, was inexperienced in this sort of thing. Old Mrs Mallett cursed the stiffness of her pins; but lurking in a summerhouse was not like sitting in a pub with a small port.

Dan took his bicycle, without lights, Natasha on the pillion.

Her hair was covered up. All they had to watch for was car headlights.

As they went, Dan felt a fresher breeze on his cheek, from a new direction. He smelled rain; by the time they were creeping into the garden of the Monk's House, he felt the first drops. As they picked their way through a belt of elderly rhododendrons the first flash of lightning flickered somewhere over Milchester. Thunder crashed, and the heavens opened. Dan was wearing cotton shirt and trousers, Natasha cotton trousers of Dan's, a blouse of his mother's, and her own canvas sneakers: light, thin clothes for the warm evening, which were within seconds saturated by the teeming black rain, and clinging to their bodies.

There were thirty yards of rough grass and a few flowering trees between the rhododendrons and the summerhouse; they crawled, because of the lightning. They had plenty of time, and the wet grass made them no wetter.

They reached the back of the summerhouse. Dan peeped round the corner, waiting for the next bolt of lightning. It came, much closer, hissing through the dense rain, illuminating for a split second the ugly bulk of the Monk's House and the lawns and shrubberies between. No one was visible. Aidan Winfrey would wait until the worst of the downpour had passed. Dan's mental clock said it was only 10.20, but he thought the colossal crashes of thunder might have put it slow or fast. He waited for the next flash, and then immediately pulled Natasha up the three creaking steps of the summerhouse, the creaking inaudible in the pounding of the rain on the asbestos roof.

Dan embraced Natasha, for the first time in what seemed a very long time. She was passive, and then active. She returned his embrace. Assisted somehow by the thunderstorm, they had moved into a new phase. They admitted to themselves – they tacitly admitted to one another – that they felt strongly about one another. And they almost trusted one another. Dan thought the next phase would be complete trust, and either that would happen because they made love, or they would make love because that happened.

Natasha felt warm, and skinny in her clinging clothes. Her hair under his hand was glued by water to her head.

Natasha was trembling in Dan's arms. She was not cold, but frightened of the thunder. Dan thought fleetingly of his dogs huddled in their kennels, Goldie the Jack Russell terrier hating the thunder and trembling as Natasha was trembling.

Still the rain teemed, thudding like something solid on the summerhouse roof. The thunderstorm seemed to have travelled fast to this spot, and then to have stuck.

Aidan Winfrey would probably tell his wife he had left a book in the summerhouse, or left a window of his car open. Still, he would wait until the worst of the storm had passed. Dan continued to embrace Natasha, because it felt nice to hold her small saturated body, and because although she felt warm she might catch cold. He looked over her shoulder out over the drenched garden. There were lights in all three flats of the house, glowing behind blinds or curtains.

A figure was visible for a split second in the lightning, crossing the grass towards the summerhouse, passing the overgrown shrubbery in which whitethroats nested; in the lightning the figure seemed to shine like a lamp, wet shiny oilskins reflecting the glare in the sky. From the rolling walk Dan recognized Aidan Winfrey. He was playing at being a squire even in the dark, even in this rain. He was twenty yards from the summerhouse.

There was another flash. To Dan's surprise, Aidan Winfrey stopped and turned, facing the shrubbery which was six feet from where he stood, a tangle of untrimmed lilac and forsythia and viburnum. It was as though somebody had called to him from the shrubbery.

Someone had. In the crash of thunder which followed close on the lightning, Dan thought he heard another crash. Aidan Winfrey was knocked over backwards, as though punched on the jaw.

The crash just audible under the crash of thunder came from a twelve-bore shotgun, and Aidan Winfrey had been hit in the chest at point-blank range.

6

Dan tried to chase whoever had fired the shotgun. He knew it was no good, in the darkness and the pounding rain, but he had to try.

It was no good.

Beyond the shrubbery, on one side, was a lane. The killer could have scrambled out of the tangle of bushes on to the lane, and disappeared safely away, in either direction, into the teeming darkness. Or crossed a strip of grass to the back of the house: all three flats had back doors on this side. Or gone round the house, with then a hundred options.

Footprints? Dan supposed there would be footprints in the damp earth of the shrubbery. Maybe the rain would wash them away; maybe they would be sheltered by the shrubs, and so preserved. If the killer had any sense he would have borrowed somebody else's gumboots and worn gloves when he pulled them on and pulled them off.

Dan approached the body gingerly. He was sure Aidan Winfrey must be dead, having taken a charge from a twelve-bore full in the chest, but for humane reasons it was necessary to make sure.

Lightning flared on the body, which lay on its back six feet from the shrubbery. It had no chest, simply a black cavity lined with shreds of oilskin. Rain hissed into the horrible wound; there was something extra pathetic, extra ghastly about the poor corpse exposed to the streaming rain.

Another flash of lightning gleamed on something shiny in the edge of the shrubbery: a double tube of metal. It was the shotgun. The killer had dropped it and run. It was borrowed or stolen, then; it would carry the owner's fingerprints but not the killer's.

Natasha in the summerhouse was crying. She had not seen

Aidan Winfrey shot, because she had been standing in Dan's arms, facing away from the garden, with her face in Dan's neck. But she had seen the body by successive flashes of lightning, and she knew what had happened.

Dan tried to comfort her, and she was a little comforted.

'We'd better get out of this,' said Dan.

'We can't just leave him there, out in the rain.'

'I know what you mean. But we can't take him with us. He can't get any wetter. Nor can we. Somebody may tip somebody off, and us being found hereabouts would be a very bad idea. As it is, nobody knows we were anywhere near the place.'

'Your mother knows where we were going.'

'When anybody asks her questions, she goes stone deaf. Miraculous, really. Hearing unimpaired as soon as they've gone.'

They went away immediately, in spite of the rain, because a garden with a corpse in it was no place to be and because Dan wanted the rain to wash away all trace of their having been there.

The rain eased as they rode home. Soon there were only a few intermittent drops, but, as it seemed to Dan was always the case after a thundershower, those few drops were ten times the normal size.

Natasha clutched him round his saturated waist. He felt her saturated bosom in his back. He thought she was comforting herself, by holding him so tight, after the shock of the murder and the awesomeness of the storm.

'Aidan Winfrey *didn't* murder the old lady, then,' Dan said.

'But he did get the money. Some money, anyway. Whatever he'd already given Sharron, and I suppose another £500.'

'Yes. He knew who did do the murder.'

'Then he was here, not in Milchester.'

'He came to the Monk's House after his wife told him about the money. He came for the money. But the murderer got there first, and Mrs Addison got there second.'

'And he got there just in time to see everything. Oh.'

Natasha's clutch grew suddenly much tighter, so that Dan had difficulty pedalling. Probably she was cold, as well as horrified; he was warm because he was working, but she was just sitting in the wind, in soaking thin clothes. Dan set himself neither to fall off nor to be dragged off.

'It's obvious that whoever murdered Mrs Addison also murdered Aidan Winfrey,' said Natasha. 'Either for fear of being found out, or because Aidan Winfrey was blackmailing them.'

'Yes, that fits.'

'But how on earth did the murderer know that Aidan Winfrey was coming to meet us?'

'Hum. From Aidan Winfrey. Must have been. Aidan Winfrey got the call he thought was Sharron asking for money, went to the murderer an' said he wanted another five hundred –'

'Where?'

'Anywhere. He had plenty of time, all evening. Golf Club, anywhere in Milchester, anywhere in Medwell, any point between. So all we have is a stolen shotgun without any fingerprints, the prints of a pair of stolen gumboots that won't ever be seen again, an' thirty million suspects instead of just one. Depressing, that.'

'Can we find out where Aidan Winfrey went after we talked to him? Who he saw?'

'The bluebottles can, I suppose. They will, I suppose. But even for them, there may be an hour or more that can't be accounted for. Winfrey can't say where he was, an' the murderer won't say, an' nobody else knows. In fact the murderer must have made sure nobody knew that he and Aidan Winfrey had had a chat.'

'I wonder,' said Natasha, 'if he said anything in the Golf Club, after the call?'

'He said something, sure. But I bet he didn't say, "That was the bird I'm having an affair with, an' she's blackmailing me 'cos I don't want my wife to find out, but it's okay about the money 'cos *I'm* blackmailing the bloke who killed the old lady last week."'

'Even if he had said all that,' said Natasha, 'we still wouldn't know who he was blackmailing . . . That murderer will have got very wet tonight.'

'So will a lot of other people. Us, for example. Anybody can get caught in the rain, specially in a thunderstorm rushing up out of nowhere.'

'Yes. What do we do now?'

'I daresay my mother will suggest something,' said Dan.

Old Mrs Mallett said, 'A-knew ye'd make muddles, wi'out me t'help. Goen after the wrong man, an' letten un be killed.'

Mrs Rose Winfrey took it pretty well.

She had not known, she said when they brought her the news in the morning, that her husband had gone out into the rain. She had not known about the rain. She had gone to bed earlier than usual, with her sleeping-pill, and the next she knew was the policewoman being as tactful as possible.

Aidan Winfrey had made a number of telephone calls during the evening after his return from the Golf Club. Rose Winfrey did not know to whom, or what was said. He said nothing to her about making arrangements to meet anybody.

Nothing was found on the body, or in the dead man's effects, which cast any light on the affair. No money was found on the body. Either he had been carrying none, or he had been robbed after his death. Robbery seemed an unlikely motive for the murder.

The girl who had answered the telephone in the Golf Club secretary's office said that the caller had had a ladylike voice, and was perhaps young. The barman, who had picked up the extension telephone, confirmed this. Neither the barman nor any of the people who were in the bar could remember anything about Aidan Winfrey's conversation on the telephone. Nobody had made an effort to listen. Everybody had, in effect, made an effort not to listen.

It could be assumed, the police said, that Aidan Winfrey had made an appointment to meet somebody, though it was impossible to say where the appointment was to have been, or with whom. Nothing else was likely to have got him out of doors at 10.30 on such a filthy night. Either the appointment was with the killer, or the killer knew about the appointment and knew what route Aidan Winfrey would take.

Nothing linked the new murder with that of Mrs Addison, except that they had taken place within a week of each other, and within fifty yards of each other. If there was a link, it might be that Aidan Winfrey had known something about Mrs Addison's death. But what could he have known, having been in London at the time? *Had* he in fact been in London at the time?

His widow said that when he went to London he stayed not at a hotel or club, which was too expensive, but with one or other of various friends or business contacts. She knew none of these people and was not sure of their names. This might sound odd, but it was so. She was too poorly to meet a lot of people, or memorize a list of names which meant nothing to her. To nobody else in the Monk's House, the village, or the Golf Club had Aidan Winfrey mentioned where he stayed in London. It was thus possible that he had been in Medwell on the night of Mrs Addison's death, and that he had been threatening, perhaps blackmailing, the murderer.

The shotgun, abandoned at the edge of the shrubbery, was the property of young Mr Guy Heron. It had been stolen eight months previously from the back of his car. He had reported the theft to the police, and claimed and received the insurance money. The theft had occurred when the car was parked behind the Chestnut Horse. Commonsense thus strongly suggested that the murderer of Aidan Winfrey was a local man, as it suggested that the murderer of Mrs Addison was a local man; and it suggested that the murders were indeed linked, and that it was the same murderer.

It was noted that the young person calling herself Natasha Chapman, whom the police urgently wished to question, had not been in Medwell when Guy Heron's shotgun was stolen. But she could have got it, by purchase or theft or loan or gift, from somebody who was in the village at the time.

Dan Mallett, taken once more into custody for questioning, denied having stolen a gun from the back of a car. There was no way he could be accused of a crime which several hundred men could have committed. But it was evident to him that he was thought the most likely person to have committed it; and that he was quite likely to have shot Aidan Winfrey with the gun, because Aidan Winfrey knew he had also killed Mrs Addison, because she had seen him robbing Lady Dodds-Freeman. That was the way, Dan thought, the bluebottles' minds were working, and he didn't blame them at all. His own mind would have worked the same way.

Their minds were working in another way too, at the same time: he was the accomplice of the woman Natasha Chapman, who answered the description of the person seen entering Lady Dodds-Freeman's flat, and who had created a strong presumption of her own guilt by disappearing. This was also, as Dan saw, a thoroughly convincing scenario. He pointed out to the police, in diffident half-way-yokel, that Sharron Syme could not possibly have seen anybody in the light from Rose Winfrey's bedroom window as late as eleven at night.

This had the effect not of making things better for Natasha, but of making them worse for himself. He was confessing that he prowled around the Monk's House late at night, as a regular thing. It was true that he broke no law by doing so, that he did work in the garden at the place, and that he was not known to have pinched anything from any of the flats. But prowling around other people's houses at eleven at night was not an honest man's way of behaving; it was Dan Mallett's way of behaving; it confirmed the bluebottle's view of Dan, and increased their reluctance to release him.

The whole thing greatly increased their desire to get their hands on Natasha.

Sharron Syme kept quiet. Dan went into Milchester to have a peek at her. If she was heartbroken at Aidan Winfrey's death, she showed no sign of it. Nobody knew she was more than a casual acquaintance of Winfrey's – he was just one among dozens of gentlemen whose hair she shampooed and who afterwards bought her a drink.

Dan thought it was barely possible that she knew whom Aidan Winfrey had been blackmailing, if that theory was right; but blankly impossible that she would come out and say so.

From the beginning, it had been tempting to suspect the doorstep dealer who had given Lady Dodds-Freeman £5,000, and who might have come back to collect it, and who might have picked up a key on the kitchen table. The idea must have occurred to the police, and they must have satisfied themselves that the gentlemen from Heritage Antiques had not stolen any money or bashed any old ladies on the head.

It had also been tempting to suspect Guy Heron, who was said to be some sort of problem, and who was at least partly an outsider. An outsider with inside knowledge. Mrs Addison had told her sister on the telephone, the afternoon before her own death, about the silver and the money. Mrs Heron might easily have told her son. They had both been in London, but he had a fast car.

Would he bash his own aunt on the head? Some men Dan knew would cheerfully bash their aunts on the head even if they weren't being caught in the act of robbery.

Perhaps his shotgun never had been stolen. He'd simply hidden it, reported it lost, and pocketed the insurance money. It was quite a normal trick; Dan knew nobs, like Mr Calloway of Woodbines, who did very well out of their houses being burgled.

Guy Heron might use his mother as an alibi if he were ever suspected. Probably she would perjure herself to protect him, as Dan's own mother certainly would do. Perhaps he already had been questioned and had accounted for his movements on the nights of both murders. If his mother was his alibi both times . . .

Dan asked Natasha about Guy Heron.

'He seems all right to me,' said Natasha, surprised. 'A bit flash. You know, dressing the part and putting on the act. He's like everybody else I've met in advertising agencies.'

'Would he bash his auntie on the head with a gin-bottle?'

'Oh no. I think he might want to, quite badly, if she saw him stealing and he knew she'd give him away, but I don't think he'd have the guts.'

'Charming mixture.'

'Just like about 99 per cent of the human race.'

'He might not have the guts in the ordinary way, but suppose he panicked and lashed out? That would be like anyway 95 per cent of the human race.'

'Including you?'

'The situation would never arise,' said Dan in his banker's voice.

'I've just thought of something,' said Natasha. 'If Aidan Winfrey wasn't the murderer but just saw what happened, or somehow knew what happened, why did that horrible Sharron tell those lies?'

'Because if the real murderer were caught, then Aidan Winfrey wouldn't be able to blackmail him any more. Sharron was lying to protect her lovely new source of income.'

'Yes, I suppose that makes sense. It seems to me that the murderer was going to kill Aidan Winfrey anyway, sooner or later. So we don't need to feel guilty that we got him shot.'

'A mite.'

'Yes. Standing in the rain and shooting somebody. I can't fit that to Guy Heron.'

'He would have been saving his neck. Saving however much more money Aidan Winfrey was going to ask him for.'

'Which was however much more money Sharron Syme was going to ask *him* for. Why couldn't she have done both murders?'

'Rotten basis for blackmailing somebody,' said Dan, 'doing murders yourself.'

'Oh. Hum. Sharron might take over and start blackmailing Guy Heron herself.'

'I doubt it. Poor life expectancy in that job, seemingly.'

'Ye ben a fine one t'talk about jobs,' said Dan's mother, who had not been attending closely.

Dan had no defensible reason for suspecting Guy Heron. If the lad had had motive and opportunity, so had countless others. He was guided only by an obscure instinct, which was highly unsatisfactory. However, he had nothing whatever else to guide him, so until he had a better idea he let the instinct take over.

He examined Natasha about Guy Heron. She could tell him

much about Guy's breed of advertising executive, but not much about him as a distinct individual which, indeed, she scarcely regarded him as being. Dan was unable to make much sense of what Natasha told him, not because she was not sensible, but because the whole world she was describing – a world of conferences, videos, wine-bars and professional intrigue – was so far outside his experience that it might have been on Borneo or Mars. It was not only a far cry from the hedgerows and coverts of Medwell Fratrorum, but also a cry equally far from the glamourless respectability of the bank in Milchester. Guy Heron did not come alive to him, in Natasha's account. He could not guess at motives, habits or sins.

Then the sports-car reappeared outside the Monk's House; it was reported, credibly enough, that Guy Heron had been given a few days off to support his mother in this difficult and tragic time.

(Mrs Rose Winfrey, who might have been expected to need far more support, seemed to need far less. She was either very brave, or very heartless, or relieved at the removal of her husband.)

Dan was able to observe this new suspect at which his instinct was illogically pointing, although Natasha said he was wasting his time.

The clothes were, Dan supposed, trendy (a word he had never had occasion to use before). The hair was moderately long. The shoes had little chains across the instep. When Guy Heron wore a tie it was a very broad tie; when he was tieless his shirt was unbuttoned to the waist. He had a face like a ferret, and a high voice. His shoulders were narrow but his hips broad. He did not look a man who would ever conceivably have owned a shotgun; presumably he had inherited it. Presumably he made plenty of money, in his trendy London job. There was no way of telling, by looking at him, why he was a problem, or what sort of problem he was.

Dan observed him watching his mother working in her garden while he himself was in a deck-chair with a gin and tonic. Something could be made of that, but not much.

Dan observed him paying for a drink in the Chestnut Horse with a twenty-pound note. Something could be made of that, since Lady Dodds-Freeman's silver had been bought with twenty-pound notes, but not much.

Dan observed him playing bar billiards in the pub with a bloke who worked on the *Milchester Argus*. Guy Heron cheated. Could anything be made of that?

Dan bicycled home slowly from the Chestnut Horse, pondering the topic of Guy Heron. He was a 'problem'. If he had lived on the other side of the world, according to his late aunt, his mother would have been able to contribute her share of the housekeeping. Her money went to him instead, then; that no doubt was the 'problem'. He was idle and selfish. He had £20 notes. He cheated in a game in which the stakes could hardly be more than the price of a drink. Speaking generally of the type to which he belonged, Natasha said he was incapable of premeditated murder. But the murder of Mrs Addison was not premeditated; it was an act of blind panic. It all fitted pretty well, even to his shotgun killing Aidan Winfrey. Maybe it fitted too well.

It would be highly interesting to know where Guy Heron had been on the night his aunt was killed. Obviously the bluebottles already did know, or thought they knew. Probably, if any of this was right, they thought he had been with his mother, because she had told them so.

Guy Heron had been given an extra holiday – compassionate leave – to look after his mother. He did it by drinking gin while she dug in the garden, and playing bar billiards in the Chestnut Horse. To be fair, she did not seem to need much looking after. She was more than ever like a hospital matron – solemn, but accustomed to horrors: putting tragedy behind her and getting on with her life.

Of course, the murder of Aidan Winfrey was premeditated. There were people who could have lashed out at poor old Mrs Addison with a gin-bottle, who could not have sat waiting in a shrubbery in a thunderstorm and then have blown a hole in that silly man's chest. That took a bit of guts, as well as cold-bloodedness. It was not very credible of the trendy advertising man Dan had been trying to observe.

Guy Heron seemed to be staying indefinitely on the spot. Maybe his firm was quite happy without him. It meant that he was there to be trapped, if there were any way to trap him, and if there were anything to trap him for.

Dan was depressed by the vagueness of his guesses and the impossibility of confirming them. The only good thing about a situation otherwise odious was that Natasha was staying in the cottage. It was still amazing, but it was nice.

All the time they were nearer to trusting one another, which seemed to be the ingredient that was needed. There had been moments when Dan thought they had arrived, but Natasha made it clear that they had not. She did not have to fight him off, because he was never one for pawing; it was done by the look on her face.

Dan hoped this would not go on for ever. It already seemed to have been going on for ever.

He turned into the track by the wood. A police car was parked outside the cottage. Dan collapsed off his bicycle into a clump of bracken, and pulled the bicycle into cover after him.

It was annoying, no worse than that. Natasha would not have been caught napping; and his mother would be acting stone-deaf, illiterate and senile. The bluebottles would wait for him, and he would wait for them, and it would all be exactly as it had been so many times.

Dan hid his bicycle in the lush midsummer undergrowth, and began to crawl round behind the cottage to where he thought Natasha would be hiding.

She was there, waiting for him, in a sandy hole under the roots of a tree. She was wearing a pair of Dan's corduroy trousers, and a black satin blouse of his mother's. She looked absurd and sweet.

'I've bogged it,' she said.

'They didn't see you?'

'They saw my bra and pants.'

'But not on you.'

'On the line. Drying. Nobody would think they were your mother's.'

Dan had seen the tiny, emerald-green bikini pants on the washing-line before. No: the thickest bobby in the world would not associate such a garment with old Mrs Mallett. Or with anybody in the village. They were big-city pants. They were the pants of a London tart, currently suspected of robbery and murder, recently supposed hiding in Reading but now revealed to be hiding in Dan's cottage.

'Now they know you're sheltering me,' said Natasha. 'You're in just as much trouble as I am.'

'A mite of trouble.'

'I'm terribly sorry. It was a bloody silly thing to do. I've bogged everything.'

'Got to dry things you wash,' said Dan.

It was true that she had been bloody silly; but there was no point in saying so. The thing was to decide where to go, and then to go there.

7

It was necessary to go a certain distance, in order to keep out from under the large and numerous feet of the bluebottles. It was important to go no further than was necessary, in order to keep in touch with events. It was desirable to have a roof, a bed or beds, running water, food, and changes of clothes.

An unoccupied nobs' house, thought Dan, with constant hot water and a well-stocked deep freeze.

At Woodbines, the bijou cottage-plus residence of Mr and Mrs Calloway, at present in Greece and there for another week, the telephone was a valuable bonus. Probably the Calloways had asked PC Gundry to keep an eye on the place, but with murders almost daily all over the parish, Jim Gundry would be preoccupied. Anyway Dan backed himself against the old killjoy.

Natasha had qualms about squatting in a stranger's house. Using the telephone, and only for a local call, was one thing. What Dan proposed troubled her reawakened Surbiton conscience. But her folly, leaving bra and pants on the washing-line, had put her in a weak debating position. That they had to go away somewhere was definitely her fault.

Dan told her that Edwin Calloway was a snob, a coward, and a crook; she should have no compunction about drinking his gin, while sitting on his sofa, while his food was cooking in his oven. Natasha did her best to fight down her compunction and, when they went to bed in the Calloways' bed, pretty well succeeded.

This move had been accomplished almost without words. It was simply something which it was time to do.

Natasha did not know how she knew this, or how Dan knew

she knew. But there was no doubt in her mind, and, seeing this, none in his.

Nothing had prepared her for such an hour.

She had expected Dan to be an ardent but bashful lover; she saw in him much promise, but she thought he would benefit from her metropolitan sophistication. Actually she was not very experienced and not at all sophisticated, but being in the village had made her seem so to herself. She was going to be kind to Dan; she was going to teach him; she was going to give him the night of his life, because that was the point they had reached.

What she found was a kind of passionate gentleness more moving and exciting than anything she had ever experienced; and she cried with joy.

As they lay in one anothers' arms, it turned out as Dan had foretold. Full trust came to them both. Dan told Natasha about the Coxens' horse, because he knew now, at last, that she would never tell anybody. Natasha told Dan about the photographs.

Having seen her body at last, he was curious to see the photographs. But she blushed, in the dark, at the memory of the photographs.

Old Mrs Mallett was adamant in her refusal to see, hear, speak or move. When the policemen showed her Natasha's disgraceful little smalls, she gibbered at them wordlessly. She was too old and too crazy to know what they were or care what they were. She reacted with a senile croak to the proposition that she had been harbouring a fugitive from justice. She quite enjoyed herself, but it all went on too long.

A detective-sergeant who had been there before (the one who looked like a Hereford bullock) finally cooked her supper. They took the police car away, late in the evening, though two of them stayed behind in the cottage. The point of that, presumably, was to lay a trap for Dan and Natasha. As well dig a hole in the ground and hope to catch a couple of spiders. Meanwhile it was lucky Dan had Natasha looking after him. She would keep him out of trouble and see that he brushed his teeth. It was bound to lead to an engagement, and then Dan would be back in the bank before he knew what had happened to him.

With signs and screeches, Mrs Mallett told the policemen to let the dogs out for a run, and to shut up the bantams in their coop. Then she took herself to bed. She let the sergeant help her upstairs, but she slammed her bedroom door in his face. She missed Natasha, so cheerful and nimble and kind, so respectable and dainty.

She lay in bed at last, wondering how to unmask and entrap the murderer before Dan made any more muck-ups and got anybody else killed. The young man from London seemed likely enough. Mrs Mallett had never, as far as she knew, met a young man from London, but she imagined him clearly enough. Time was, she had read many a good story in the little books they sold at the newsagent's in the village, where men from London arrived in fast cars and took advantage of innocent country girls. If they had little black moustaches, they were finally hit on the chin by the young squire. If they had fair hair, naturally wavy, they turned out to be dukes in disguise, and they won the milkmaid's love. Mrs Mallett made a mental note to ask Natasha whether this Guy Heron had a little black moustache or wavy fair hair.

The noise did not wake Natasha; she was already awake. She was lying on her side, facing Dan, in the Calloways' double bed, which had a very comfortable mattress and very soft and numerous pillows. Dan was breathing softly. It was impossible to imagine him snoring, or shifting restlessly, or moaning or dribbling in his sleep. Everything he did, Natasha thought, he did with a kind of elegance, with what her mother called good breeding. That was funny, for he was a poacher and the son of a poacher, and his strange, rather sweet old mother couldn't be called anything but a peasant. Yet he acted better bred than somebody like Lady Dodds-Freeman who was a genuine sort of minor-league aristocrat, and who was a shameless old lush.

The night was fine, but there was no moon. The curtains and the window were open, which might have been risky in bright moonlight, but probably they would have taken the risk; neither Dan nor Natasha could bear sleeping in an airless room. The window was an oblong only a little paler than the surrounding darkness. Nothing else could be seen at all, not even Dan, whose soft breath she could feel on her cheek. She badly wanted to touch him, but she knew that he would wake instantly, alert even in sleep.

At bedtime they had shared a bath. Natasha had never shared a bath with a man before, but she was sure Dan had shared a bath with a girl. He had done all kinds of things with all kinds of girls, including the horrible Sharron Syme, and part of Natasha was sick at the thought of all those girls, and part was still amazed at the gentle, passionate sophistication of his love-making, which would presumably not have been possible without a good many of those girls. She mocked herself for the presumption with which she had told herself that she would give Dan a lovely lesson.

She was thinking of the lesson which she had, in the event, been given, when she heard the car. It was the first car she had heard. She supposed the road by the house went somewhere. The car was coming towards the house; the noise of the engine grew louder. It was being driven quite slowly. She thought she saw a glow of headlights. She waited for the car to go past the house, and on to wherever it was going.

The car slowed, and changed gear. The glare of its headlights washed across the open oblong of the window as it turned the corner in the drive and climbed the brief slope towards the house.

Her brain half comatose with sleepiness and with love, Natasha thought first stupidly that burglars had arrived; then that the police had arrived. It could not be the owners of the house; they were in Greece. Dan had said so, and Dan was now to be believed implicitly about everything.

The car crunched to a halt on gravel immediately below the window. A door opened. A man's voice said something Natasha could not catch. The voice sounded angry and exhausted, the voice of a man whose holiday has been cut short, and who has driven a long way at night.

Natasha shook Dan. He was fully awake, immediately, without sound. He sat up in bed, still invisible to Natasha in the darkness.

'Let's leave the heavy stuff in the car,' said a woman's voice in a suffering tone. 'The overnight things are on top. I want to be in bed in three minutes.'

'Gum,' murmured Dan. 'Take the bulbs out of the bedside lights.'

Natasha nodded, at the same time realizing that this was purposeless in the dark. Dan slid out of bed. He pulled a stool from the dressing-table to the middle of the room. Natasha could just see him now. Standing on the stool, he took the bulb from the ceiling light.

As Natasha took the bulbs from the bedside lamps, she heard the unlocking of the front door, and then footsteps clumping below.

Natasha got out of bed and went to the window. The night air was cool on her naked body. The big car was parked by the front door, all four doors open and the interior light on. A middle-aged couple were going to and fro, taking things from the car to the house.

Natasha groped about for her clothes. She remembered that they had all come off in the sitting-room downstairs, and that they were still there, disgracefully strewn on the carpet. There were not many of them; her only underclothes were still on the line outside the cottage. Dan's clothes were there, too. In a moment the owners of the house would go into the sitting-room and see them.

There was a shriek from downstairs. It was the shriek of a woman who has seen a lot of clothes strewn on the floor of her sitting-room. Then there was the shriek of a woman who has seen dirty plates and glasses on her kitchen draining-board. Then there was the yell of a man who has seen the door of his drink-cupboard open, and a new bottle of whisky no longer new.

Natasha tried the door of the wardrobe. It was locked. There was no key.

She remembered that the house had only one staircase, which went down into the hall under a brilliant overhead light. The foot of the staircase was beside the sitting-room door and opposite the kitchen door.

'Other bedrooms, bathroom, all traps,' murmured Dan. 'Sorry about this.'

Downstairs there was still incoherent bellowing. Natasha thought, for an idiotic moment, that she now knew what noise the three bears had made when they came home and found that Goldilocks had eaten their porridge.

Dan opened the bedroom door. The light from the hall below moderately lit the passage. Dan carried the stool out into the passage. Natasha was startled, for another moment of equal idiocy, to be reminded that he was naked as she was. He stood on the stool, and took the bulb out of the passage light.

The upstairs passage was by no means in total darkness – if it had been even a little darker, Dan would not have looked so disgracefully unseemly, stretching up to unscrew the bulb. But to anybody coming up from the brilliantly lit hall, it would be pretty hard to see.

Dan brought the stool back into the bedroom. He sped, as though he could see in the dark, to the bedside table on which there was an extension telephone. He took the receiver off, and put it down gently beside the table. Until it was spotted and replaced, no calls could be made from either of the telephones downstairs, and incoming calls would get an 'engaged' signal.

There was a telephone ping, audible from downstairs. From the unhooked bedroom extension came the grating noise of dialling. Mr Calloway was in too emotional a state to notice that his telephone had no dialling tone. There were three long churrs as he dialled; he was dialling 999; he was trying to get the police. He shouted that the telephone was out of order, and that he was going to have a look round upstairs. His wife bleated at him to be careful. He said he would be careful. There was a rattling, as of a bag of golf-clubs. He was doing what Natasha's father would have done – had done, several times, when her mother imagined burglars: he was arming himself with a golf-club.

He began thumping upstairs.

Dan pulled Natasha into the lee of the wardrobe, the blackest part of a room no longer, to her eyes, completely black. They stood squashed together in the corner made by wardrobe and wall, as though they were playing nudist sardines.

At the top of the stairs Mr Calloway clicked the switch of the passage light. He swore. He clicked it up and down half a dozen times, as people always do, though if a switch does not work at once it will not work at all. He blundered to the open door of the bedroom. He clicked the switch of the overhead light. He swore again.

From the top of the stairs he yelled, 'Where's the torch?'

'In the kitchen,' quavered Mrs Calloway's voice from below. 'I'll get it.'

Mr Calloway started downstairs.

Dan nipped out of the corner, and once again picked up the stool from the dressing-table. He opened the window to its fullest extent and dropped the stool on to the roof of the car below. Natasha winced at the clang.

'Do they both go out?' murmured Dan, peeping out of the window. 'Yes. Quick.'

They ran downstairs and across the hall, under the glare of its brass chandelier. Through the open front door, Natasha glimpsed the Calloways crooning over their car. The woman was in profile. She might have seen, from the corner of her eye, two glaringly visible naked persons sprinting across her hall.

Natasha deeply wanted to run into the sitting-room to retrieve her clothes, but this was of all moves the least possible.

Dan opened another door off the hall, pulled her in behind him, and shut the door. In the glimmer of light coming in from outside, Natasha saw that they were in a dining-room with a polished table and a sideboard and half a dozen chairs. Dan pulled a chair to a window. He reached up, and began fiddling with something behind the pelmet of the curtain. Natasha found time to wonder why on earth he was fixing the Calloways' pelmet: as some sort of compensation for the atrocities they had committed?

Dan unscrewed the little clamps at each end of the curtain-rail. He pushed the curtains, outwards, off the rail, so that they ballooned on to the floor.

'Fig-leaves,' said Dan. 'Brocade sarongs.'

Natasha giggled, with at least as much hysteria as amusement, and wound the stiff curtain round herself. It would stay in place only if she held it. She felt more civilized but less mobile; she could, of course, always take it off if they had to run away very fast.

Dan opened the window and climbed out of it. He had not yet

put on his sarong. He was right; Natasha's fell off as she followed him out of the window. It was as she was scrambling through, trailing the curtain, that the dining-room door burst open and the light came on. Natasha shot off the windowsill and into a flowerbed. It had been well mulched with some sort of sticky compost. Natasha was aware, even in the crisis of the moment, that the mulch was grass-mowings and not manure. Dan pulled her to her feet, and picked up her curtain. It caught itself on a spiny plant; when he yanked, the plant came too. They ran away across a lawn trailing two curtains and a small pyracantha.

Dan knew the way. Even as a figure appeared in the door of the house, running and waving a flashlight, Dan steered Natasha to a gap in a hedge, and thence through a kitchen garden to a small back gate on to the road.

'One thing I hate', said Dan, 'is people changing their plans.'

They put on their sarongs, and started back the way they had come. They kept to the metalled road, being barefoot, but ready at any moment to dive for cover. Natasha wondered what Dan's next idea would be, and what she would be wearing when they escaped from that.

She said, 'I feel rather awful about all that damage.'

'What damage? If they can afford a holiday in Greece, they can afford a bite of food for fugitives.'

'Well, these curtains.'

'To be returned, of course. By that time he will have claimed on his insurance, and he'll have both the curtains and the cost of new ones. He'll love that. He's always doing it. Some people collect stamps; Mr Edwin Calloway collects insurance money.'

'What did you do to his car?'

'It's not his car. It's one of those perks they talk about. I bet your father gets a company car.'

'Well, yes.'

'And he pays for the petrol, and the company pays for repairs?'

'Well, yes.'

'There you are then. I don't think the stool was damaged. Even if it wasn't, I bet he claims for the cost of a new one.'

'You're really just saying all that because you feel a bit guilty.'

'Hum,' said Dan. 'Well, we don't need dinner. You do need another bath. We want somewhere to lay our heads.'

'And I suppose we'd better have some clothes.'

'Why? Very fetching, a sarong. Puts you in mind of coconuts and rum punch.'

'I hate the taste of coconut,' said Natasha, bursting out laughing in spite of herself.

In fact she found her sarong so awkward and uncomfortable that she took it off, and carried it over one shoulder like a Scotsman's plaid. She thought that walking naked down a public road was the oddest thing she had ever done. The sarong could be resumed if decency were required. Meanwhile there was no need for decency in the dark, and none with Dan.

'At an earlier stage,' said Dan, 'we were wondering what house we could get into. That was so you could be Sharron Syme on the telephone.'

How that damned girl's name did keep cropping up, thought Natasha.

'The Calloways' was the only one,' said Dan. 'We don't want to go miles away; we just can't lose touch. Anyway we don't want to travel in sarongs. We can't go home, for the bluebottles are sure to be camping there for a bit. There ought to be an empty house, this time of the year, but there just isn't.'

'Isn't there anybody we could trust to hide us? . . . No, silly question.'

'Is there anybody we could trust not to see us?'

'You mean somebody blind?' said Natasha, shocked.

'Blind to the world.'

'Lady Dodds-Freeman.'

'I wouldn't fancy sleeping there, scene of a murder an' all. It doesn't seem to bother her, because she never really took in what happened. Anyway, it's one place I never had a key to.'

'Rose Winfrey's just as blind to the world, zonked on those sleeping pills.'

Dan stopped dead, as though he had walked into a pane of plate-glass across the road.

'Never struck me that was possible,' he said. 'Is it possible?'

'Have you got a key to that flat?'

'I can lay my hands on one. I haven't got one in my waistcoat pocket at this moment.'

'Why?'

'Now that,' said Dan mildly, 'I do call a silly question.'

'I mean, why did you ever want a key to the Winfreys' flat?'

'Habit, really. Automatic response to the fact of a nob's residence. You never know when a need's going to arise, or what need it's going to be. Hum. She's out to the world at this moment, yes. And I don't suppose she's an early riser, an invalid like that. You wouldn't be able to run a bath there. Water goes thrum-thrum all over the house, whenever anybody has a bath.'

'However do you know that?'

'Incessant cause o' complaint. Plumbing very casual. Scandalous, really.'

'I could sort of sponge myself.'

'You'd better leave it to me. I can reach the small of your back.'

'Clothes. Can you bring yourself to wear dead Mr Winfrey's clothes?'

'I can't see him minding, unless she's already given them all away to Oxfam.'

'Well, I can't see myself pinching any of her clothes, a helpless old thing like that.'

'Regard it as more of a loan. It's that, or the same somewhere else, or it's your sarong.'

'Now you're sold on my idea, and you're selling it to me.'

'Hum. It means a very early start in the morning. Rose Winfrey may not be an early riser, but the milkman is. So's Mrs Heron, I bet.'

'Never mind about sleep. The important thing is for me to get all this muck off me, and for us both to get some clothes.'

'Yes, we can find somewhere for a nap later in the morning. Meanwhile there's hours of darkness. It's about two now.'

'Is that all?' said Natasha, startled.

'Violent events always seem to take longer than they really do. We weren't beset by the Calloways for more than about five minutes.'

'It seemed like an hour and a half.'

'Fraught episodes, adrenalin pumping . . . I've never properly seen Rose Winfrey. I wasn't there when they arrived, an' ever since she hasn't been out of the house.'

'She's not bedridden?'

'Next kin to it. Never stirs from her sofa, so they say. A woman comes in from the village to clean up and feed her. Name of Lizzie Bunn. Widow, sour but straight. One of my detractors, actually. You've probably seen her going in and out.'

'Yes, she looks like a camel. Are you sure she never spends the night there?'

'Neither one of them would have that. Lizzie Bunn has to get back to feed her cat. She comes in about ten in the morning, so I s'pose that's when Rose Winfrey has her breakfast.'

Natasha pondered for a moment as she walked. Then she stopped dead, as suddenly as Dan had.

She said, 'That place must be haunted. Mrs Addison *and* Aidan Winfrey. I don't want to go there at night.'

'I'll protect you.'

'Yes, I know you will, but you know what I mean.'

'I do know what you mean, and if I could think of anything else I'd have thought of it.'

Natasha allowed herself to be led towards the Monk's House.

In spite of superstitious fears, and other more rational causes for alarm, it was pleasant walking through the soft night. There was no traffic on the little back roads: they never had to dive into a thorn hedge. Natasha saw the point of nudism: the caress of air on your skin, and the sense of utter freedom.

She saw the point of Dan's unorthodox precautions, when from behind a loose brick in a garage wall he produced the key of Mrs Winfrey's flat.

The flat was above Lady Dodds-Freeman's, though it was much smaller. Mrs Heron's flat was in fact a small maisonette or duplex, set beside the other two. When the house had been a house there had been, of course, connecting doors between Mrs Heron's part of the house and both the other flats. Dan did not know if these had been bricked up or merely permanently locked. It made no practical difference; there was no risk of Natasha and himself being surprised by Mrs Heron.

Rose Winfrey had her own front door, and Dan had seen the extra staircase being built from the small extra hallway of her flat. She had her own back door, too, which was quite unnecessary, but was used because it already existed. This was the door Dan had the key to.

Some instinct made Natasha put on her sarong as they neared the house. Some instinct made Dan take a wide detour round the summerhouse and the belt of shrubbery from which Aidan Winfrey had been shot.

Dan knew the general arrangement of the four rooms of the Winfreys' flat. He knew where the kitchen and bathroom were, because from a discreet distance he had watched them being installed. He knew that Mrs Winfrey's bedroom was the one at the front; this was how it was that the light from her window fell on Lady Dodds-Freeman's door, though not as late as Sharron Syme had said it did. The other three rooms were presumably Aidan Winfrey's bedroom (it was doubtful if they had shared a room, her health being what it was and her hours early as they were), a sitting-room, and a dining-room or study or such: whatever inhospitable near-nobs would use a fourth room for. It was necessary to know which other room was which, in order to find male clothes. Female clothes would presumably only be found in Rose Winfrey's bedroom; it was to be hoped her Mogadon was good and strong.

It would not matter if floorboards creaked; Lady Dodds-Freeman would hear nothing.

To show a light would be a bad idea, just in case PC Gundry or anybody else took it into their heads to come snooping. Dan wondered how they were going to pick suitable clothes in pitch darkness, and how he was going to get the mulch off Natasha if he couldn't see where it was. That was a problem for when they were inside.

The Yale key was quite silent in the back door. There was a bolt, but as Dan knew it was never used; Lizzie Bunn came in quite properly by the back door, using her own key, which would have been impossible if the door was bolted. It was also said in the Chestnut Horse that Rose Winfrey was afraid of fire; she could get herself downstairs, somehow or other, but might not manage a struggle with a stiff old bolt.

The simple Yale lock represented no invitation to burglary: the Winfreys had nothing much worth burgling. Dan and Natasha, needing garments, were the only people in the world likely to bother Rose Winfrey in the small hours, and she would never know she had been bothered.

It occurred to Dan, as he led Natasha along the little back passage to the foot of the stairs, that at some point Mrs Winfrey would discover that things of hers and of Aidan's were missing. Who could she blame but Lizzie Bunn? That was bad. Something would have to be done about it. But it was a problem for another day.

They crept up the stairs, Dan leading. To his surprise, he became aware of a dim glow of light. He saw, as his head reached the level of the landing, that it came through the crack under Rose Winfrey's bedroom door. She slept with a nightlight, then. That was reasonable; many invalids did, so that they could find the right pills in a hurry if there were a crisis in the night, or simply for comfort. He did not think he had ever seen the glow of a nightlight, passing the Monk's House in the dark. Perhaps she had thick curtains, drawn close; perhaps she had only just taken to a nightlight.

He heard a voice. Mrs Winfrey was talking in her sleep. Did people talk in drugged sleeps? Wasn't it a sign of very light sleep, near to waking? Dan froze where he was to listen, and by squeezing her arm froze Natasha. There was an answering murmur in a man's voice. Was Mrs Winfrey doing male impersonations in her sleep?

There was a low, sexy woman's laugh. A man's soft laugh. Two dozen theories shot into Dan's head simultaneously, all blankly impossible.

Floorboards creaked, and the door suddenly opened. Rose Winfrey came out of the bedroom and walked along the passage to the kitchen. She was wearing a dressing gown; it was open at the front, and she had nothing on underneath it. She turned on the kitchen light, and Dan heard water running into a kettle.

Rose Winfrey looked to Dan about forty. She had, for her age, an excellent figure, a little on the plump side. In imagining her older, Dan had gone on Aidan Winfrey's apparent age, and on the fact of her being an invalid. She was quite small, two or three inches over five foot. Her hair was down, as well it might be. It was pale, colourless, on the way from blonde to grey, or between blonde rinses, or faded as a result of an indolent indoor life.

Rose Winfrey was not an invalid. She moved briskly. She did not glide but strode from the bathroom to the kitchen. She pretended to be an invalid, then, either because she was bone lazy, or for some other reason. More theories popped into Dan's head.

The bedroom door was half open, and Dan could not see the bed. He heard, from inside the room, the scrape of a match.

From the kitchen came the rattling of the lid of the kettle as the water boiled. There were various muted bangs and clicks, and Rose Winfrey came back along the passage with two mugs on a little tray. Dan smelled coffee. Mogadon, he thought, only came into this woman's life, if at all, when she had nothing better to do.

Rose Winfrey paused for a second at the door of the bedroom, as though making sure that she had a proper grip of the tray, so that the mugs would not slide and spill. Light from inside the room shone on her colourless hair, making it look better than it was, making her look better than she was.

Dan had the sense that he was being shown something beyond the obvious things he was being shown. But he was too astonished by all this to identify it.

Mrs Winfrey pushed open the bedroom door with her foot. It swung wide, and Dan saw the bed. Sitting on the side of it, smoking, his hair rumpled and his face cheerful, was young Mr Guy Heron.

8

Guy Heron was naked. His shoulders were narrow, his hips broad, his belly slack and plump. Rose Winfrey had the better figure, although she was a dozen years older and apparently did without any exercise. Perhaps she took exercise in secret; perhaps this was an example of regular exercise she took.

In the far wall of the room there was a door which evidently gave to the Herons' flat. It had not been bricked up. No doubt it was normally locked, from one side or the other, and bolted from one side or both. Love laughed at locksmiths. Presumably Guy Heron's bedroom was on the other side of that door.

The implications rushed at Dan, like a flock of bantams rushing at the rattle of corn in a scoop.

The first and most obvious was that the two murders might not be connected at all. Rose Winfrey might have murdered her husband because he was inhibiting her enjoyment of her young lover. Physically, it was clear, she was quite capable of doing so. Or Guy Heron might have shot Aidan Winfrey, for all sorts of readily guessable reasons. They would not have had to be told where Aidan Winfrey was going on the night of his death: Rose Winfrey could simply have listened to him talking on the telephone, probably pretending she was doped.

Guy Heron could have heard about Lady Dodds-Freeman's money not from his mother but from his mistress.

The light could, after all, have been on in Rose Winfrey's bedroom, so Sharron Syme might have seen somebody at Lady Dodds-Freeman's door.

It seemed to Dan marginally more likely that Rose Winfrey had killed Mrs Addison and Guy Heron had killed Aidan Winfrey. But it could have been the other way round. Or either of them could have done both murders. Or both could be entirely innocent – at least of murder – and either one, or two, other people, with or without accomplices, might be guilty.

The affair between Guy Heron and Rose Winfrey might be of long standing, in which case it might be highly relevant to one or both murders; or it might be a brand-new consequence of Aidan Winfrey's death, in which case it bore no relevance to the murders at all.

It was easy to see a pattern in all this. It was easy to see about three hundred patterns, none preferable to any other. Dan felt as though he was looking at a kaleidoscope being held by a palsied idiot: there was an infinity of satisfactory and symmetrical pictures constantly changing into one another.

Meanwhile Natasha still needed a wash, and they both still needed clothes.

Possibilities continued to surge into Dan's mind, which felt hyperactive and out of control. Aidan Winfrey had presumably known that his wife was no invalid: why then had he gone along with the farce? Because he was financially dependent? In order to give himself liberty for his own back-street frolics with the likes of Sharron Syme? Was it possible Rose could have fooled him?

Or could he have been blackmailing his own wife?

The bedroom door was still open. The shameless couple finished their coffee and re-embarked on intimacies which Dan had no wish to observe. There were no clothes nor wet sponges in that flat, not for them, not that night. They crept downstairs to the passage.

Natasha was now wearing her curtain as a cloak, which alternately concealed and revealed her nakedness. It was doubly incongruous that she should be deeply shocked at what they had just seen, since Aidan Winfrey was still in the morgue, unburied, at the disposal of coroner and police. The implications of an affair between Rose Winfrey and Guy Heron began to strike her, almost visibly, much as they had struck Dan.

They slipped out of the house, and Dan put the key back behind its brick.

'Is he getting something out of her?' said Natasha. 'Or is she getting something out of him? Or do they just like each other?'

'All three, maybe.'

'I suppose she got him to kill her husband?'

'But why? She's not going to marry that lad. They could have gone on as they were. If they *were* going on. Gum, what a muddle. I want a bed and some pants, in that order.'

'We need a better idea than either of your last two.'

'I've got one,' said Dan. 'Only it's putting pants and bed in the other order.'

'Pants would be a help,' said Natasha, rearranging her cloak in a way that drew attention, even in almost total darkness, to her lack of them.

'Come along, then.'

'Where are we going? I haven't quite lost faith in you, but I'm coming near it.'

'Search for raiment,' said Dan. 'The Great Pant Hunt. We'll borrow Guy Heron's car. He won't be wanting it for an hour or two.'

'Have you got the key of that too?'

'He doesn't lock it up, down here. Probably he does in London. He doesn't know how artful we are, down here in the backwoods. Full of sly tricks.'

Dan knew where Guy Heron put his car, in a kind of lean-to behind the garages. He knew where the key lived, under the rubber mat in front of the driver's seat. He had not expected to profit from the knowledge, Guy Heron being a bird of passage, his arrivals and departures unpredictable, his car often on the road. He supposed he could drive the car; he supposed he could drive any car, although he had never had a driving lesson, passed any test, or held a licence.

The car made an obtrusive snarling sound when Dan started it. He hoped the owner was thoroughly preoccupied. It turned more nimbly and accelerated more sharply than any car he was used to; gravel spun below their wheels, and they narrowly missed the towering Wellingtonia by the main gates.

'It's no good having pants if we're dead,' said Natasha. 'Wouldn't you be better with some lights?'

'Might risk them now,' agreed Dan. 'I wonder where they are.'

He turned on the windscreen wipers, the indicators, the

hazard lights, the rear-window defroster, and achieved an unnerving blare of static from the radio, before he found the lights.

'Too many buttons,' said Dan apologetically, 'as the actress said to the bishop.'

'Why did she?'

'She was taking off his gaiters.'

'That's not very funny,' said Natasha primly.

Dan drove to Milchester, becoming more accustomed to light steering and violent acceleration. In the glow of the dashboard light he could see that Natasha's face was distrustful; he did not blame her.

They had learned some startling facts, from which followed equally startling though contradictory conclusions. He rather regretted the new facts; all they did was confuse him. Probably in the morning he would see things clearer, especially if they found somewhere to sleep before them.

Dan drove to Milchester and to East Street. He parked outside Twirlies, where Sharron Syme gave blow-waves to travelling salesmen. The street was empty of people and completely quiet, with a few parked cars. The street lights were moderately bright, but there were no lights in any upstairs windows. A few shop windows were lit, advertising their wares to empty cars.

'This is idiotic,' said Natasha. 'What are you going to do, steal a hairdrier?'

Dan got out of the car. After a struggle he opened the boot, and after a search found a leather bag of tools – screwdriver, monkey-wrench, jack-handle, the hexagonal pipe for unscrewing the sparking plugs.

He led Natasha to the first plate-glass window of Ward's, the department store. There was no light in the window, and none that he could see in the depths of the shop behind. There was a fair amount of light from a street lamp opposite. The display was unchanged – the rigid, grinning dummies were dressed for holidays in gigantic hotels in Majorca.

Dan led Natasha to the next window, in which the ladies had just been swimming, or were just about to drink champagne cocktails by the pool.

'Just hope they haven't finished whatever they were doing,' murmured Dan.

They had not. The last third of the ladies' window was still boarded, and still bore its hand-lettered apology for inconvenience. The boarding included the side of the slight bow which the window formed.

Rather more light from the street-lamp flooded into the ladies' window, gleaming on long blonde wigs and pale, etiolated limbs in brilliant cotton.

'Might be a watchman, might be an alarm, might be a dog,' said Dan. 'I'll need some kind of cover, doing my carpentry.'

'The only cover we've got is what we're wearing.'

'Yes. We can hang the curtains over this bit of scaffolding. You'll have to hold them.'

'Brocade curtains in the street are going to look very peculiar.'

'It's pretty dark. Trendy tarpaulins. Not as peculiar as I'd look, burgling a shop in my birthday suit.'

Dan undraped his sarong and Natasha her cloak. Naked in a street in a town, she felt even odder than when walking down a country road. She thought it was not so much involvement with murder that had placed her in these unthinkable predicaments, but simply involvement with Dan.

Dan draped one curtain over the horizontal tube of scaffolding that ran parallel to the front of the shop, and one to the piece at right angles. He thus gave himself a small square space in which to get at the boards over the window. Natasha, also occupying the space, restricted his movements; it was really a very small space for the two of them.

'Keep a watch out through the crack between an' the cracks at both ends,' said Dan. 'I'm bound to make a bit of noise.'

'Yes. What happens if somebody comes along and looks inside our tent?'

'Then they get us for indecent exposure. It doesn't much matter, when they're after us for murder.'

Natasha saw the force of this, though she thought Dan might have put it more consolingly.

Dan set to work with screwdriver, monkey-wrench and jack-handle. They were not at all the tools he wanted, but they were the ones he had. He wanted an old-fashioned tyre-lever, a claw hammer, and a saw. The saw would perhaps have been dangerously noisy.

The screwdriver was dangerously noisy, too; when he levered a board away from the joist to which it was nailed, there was a scream like that of a cat caught in a door.

A car passed, as someone on a night shift went home or someone in a hospital went to work. There was no need for Natasha to tell Dan to stop wrenching the planks off the joists. They both froze. The car disappeared, changing gear as it turned by the Butter-Market.

'Lucky we're both skinny little runts,' said Dan, resuming his labours. 'Two planks'll do it.'

'I'm not so sure,' said Natasha, aware as seldom before of the jut of her breasts, and imagining unhappily scraping them against the splintery woodwork of a too-small gap.

She saw a moving shadow approaching on the other side of the street, and shushed Dan. The shadow was a couple, obtrusively courting. Their progress was very slow, because they kept stopping to embrace. Natasha thought they were inconsiderate, because they were interrupting for an absurdly long time the burglary of the shop, and vulgar, because they were necking in a public place.

A caress from Dan – something to occupy the time, perhaps, until he could safely proceed with business – reminded her that she was not in any posture to be priggish. But she was entitled to be impatient. If the damned couple were on their way to bed, why didn't they go? And if they weren't, why were they teasing one another in a way that couldn't be good for them?

At long, long last young love removed itself to the car-park behind the Odeon Cinema, where presumably the couple would either get into a car and go somewhere, or else get into a car and not go somewhere. Either way, Dan could get on. He got on, making so much noise from the screaming of nails coming out of wood and the rending of wood coming out of nails that Natasha could not believe that the windows of East Street remained dark.

'That's it, I hope,' murmured Dan. 'Look out for splinters.'

'Can we take the curtains?' said Natasha, looking bashfully at the broad countryside behind the shop window, visible through the gap in the boards and peopled with sporting ladies, which seemed brilliantly lit after their little cubicle, and after her eyes had got used to the dark.

'Best leave them,' said Dan. 'My carpentry would look a bit funny, if anybody came along.'

He snaked through the gap in the boards, climbed up about a yard, and emerged among the chic, frozen dummies. To Natasha, still outside in the dark, his white body looked screamingly visible and screamingly indecent among the ladies; as though some small nudist had gate-crashed a party at the Ritz.

Natasha followed, gulping, anxious about the splinters. She scrambled awkwardly up on to the floor of the window. She felt horribly public and exposed: she felt exactly as though she were making an entrance on to a well lit stage in a theatre which might, at any moment, fill up with people.

Dan was inspecting the back of the five-foot-wide space which the display occupied. He felt the partition with his hands, top to bottom and all along its length.

'Hum,' he said.

'That's usually bad news,' said Natasha.

'I'd banked on getting out of this window, maybe over a little barrier, an' having the run of the shop. But it's massive, this wall behind.'

'There must be a door in it, or how could they get in here to dress the dummies?'

'There is a door in it,' said Dan mildly. 'Feels three inches thick, an' it's locked.'

'More people being selfish,' said Natasha crossly.

Dan himself was suddenly somehow squeezed into a shadow behind a lady in a floor-length wrap-around. Natasha was in partial cover, but only partial. Two policemen, with large official flashlights, came very slowly into view in front of the window. They seemed to be in as little hurry as the courting couple. One of them said something; the other grunted in response; Natasha could hear their voices, though not what they said. One shone his flashlight in through the window at the end. The beam played up and down the lady in the sea-green caftan. The voices of the policemen rumbled; they were discussing the caftan, picturing their girlfriends in it, or failing to do so. They inspected the next dummy minutely, the beam of the powerful flashlight going from head to toe and back again. They were students of resort fashions; they were very bored, and the clothes were something to look at, something to pass the time.

The beam impaled the second lady, and the third, flaxen-haired, slender, waxy-white, stiffly posturing, in cotton and chiffon. Natasha was between the fourth and fifth ladies, and behind them. The flashlight had a narrow, concentrated beam, but still it filled the whole length of the window with reflected radiance. Natasha tried to fix on her face the fashionable pout of the dummies. She willed herself to absolute immobility. She stared blankly straight ahead. She was turned slightly away from the window, towards the back, because she had been talking to Dan when he told her to freeze. That was good. Nothing else was good, but that was. In terms of general contour, the dummies were accurate representations of live females, but not in all detail. It would have been unseemly to strive for greater accuracy; it would also have been pointless, since the very function of the dummies was to have their nakedness concealed by clothes. Natasha was fair-minded enough to recognize this with part of her mind, even as she strove not to blink or to tremble, but another part of her mind was furious with the makers of dummies for their negligent idleness.

Unclothed dummies were quite often visible in shop windows, when the window-dressers were putting on a new display. People were used to how they looked, to the marble hairlessness of bodies, to unpunctuated breasts, to visible joins which enabled arms and legs to be moved. Natasha was not a good model of a dummy, though her hair was about right and her figure was about right and her skin was about the right pale colour. If she had no lines where arms joined shoulders and legs joined hips, at least she had no bikini lines either.

The beam moved to the third lady and lingered over her terry wrap, as though caressingly. Natasha became angry. Was that what everybody paid taxes for, to have public servants spending their entire time smacking their lips over plaster of Paris dummies? Had these policemen nothing better to do? Was there no crime going on?

Natasha remembered that these policemen were, in fact, on the point of discovering a crime. They only had to move their flashlight beam a yard to the left. If they did so, it would be like being on a stage in the most brilliant solo spot. It was a thing people had nightmares about, being caught with their trousers down, in a spotlight, on a stage. Natasha had never had this nightmare, but she thought she would in the future, if she had any future.

She remembered improvisation classes at drama school when she had had to be a tree or a lamp-post. You thought yourself into it, approaching performance from inside, from feeling rather than observation. She thought herself into being plaster of Paris. But she thought her behind might be scratched from the wood in the window; and she remembered with a shock that she was still muddy from the flowerbed into which she had dived. Perhaps the mud would hide the scratches, and the absence of joins for arms and legs. She thought herself into being a dirty plaster of Paris dummy.

It was the performance of her life.

The policemen were admiring the third dummy longer than the courting couple had admired one another.

Natasha's pose, frozen in mid-movement, was stiff and unnatural. Perhaps it was dummy-like. At least it was not uncomfortable. Dan's probably was, crouched into a ball behind a skirt. If he got cramp they were lost. As an aid to remaining rigid, Natasha set herself to will Dan's limbs not to get cramp. She also willed the policemen to go away, or have fits, or drop dead.

The direct glare of the beam swung past her, and waggled safely on to the remaining dummies. They were inspected cursorily; the passion of the policemen for resort fashions had evaporated. Presently the light disappeared, and the policemen stumped away.

They paid no attention to the brocade curtains. Perhaps they did not recognize them as brocade curtains.

Natasha held her pose, rigid, until she was sure the policemen were clear away. Then she sat down suddenly between dummies, and began to giggle hysterically.

'Oscar-winning performance,' said Dan, emerging stiffly from his hiding place. 'Lucky you didn't get the full candle-power.'

'Are you sure we can't get into the shop?'

'Yes. We'll have to do with what's here.'

'You too? Oh Dan! Of course. We can't even get into the other window.'

'This bird has a pair of pants that might just about fit me.'

They were the only trousers in the window. They were very thin, made of a mixture of cotton and something with a chemical name, hugely bell-bottomed, and in colour fuchsia with lime-green stripes. They looked pretty ridiculous on the dummy; on Dan they would look grotesque. But if he wanted trousers, these were his trousers.

Dan lifted the dummy awkwardly, and Natasha eased the trousers off it. Dan put them on. They did look grotesque. He teamed them with a yellow shirt with puffed sleeves. It was not the shirt to go with those trousers; it was not the shirt for a man to wear with any trousers; but it was the only garment in the window that you could honestly call a shirt.

Natasha took a bikini and a caftan. There were no pants to be had. She found some sandals that more or less fitted her. Dan's feet were small, but not as small as those of the dummies.

Natasha took a hat; there was no hat in the window Dan could wear without exciting even more derision than the rest of his clothes.

'What's a nice, normal girl like you doing with a hippie like me?' said Dan.

'Trying to reform you,' said Natasha. 'Getting you off the hard stuff.'

They scraped their way out through the hole in the planks, careful not to tear their new finery. They decided to leave the curtains where they were, to compensate the shop for the loss of the clothes. They paused to look at the window they had looted. It had the appearance of an orgy, two dummies topless, one bottomless, and one naked except for the Caribbean scarf round her head.

'Shocking sight for the folk of the town,' said Dan. 'We'd better get out of here.'

'Where to?'

'Point for debate. I'm out of ideas. We don't have to hide quite as much as we did half an hour ago, but I don't want to be seen in public by anybody that knows me.'

They went to the car. Dan drove out of Milchester, towards Medwell. Dawn would come. Dan had not the slightest idea where to go or what to do, or how to save Natasha or himself.

9

First stop was the Monk's House. It was a pity to abandon the car, but it would have been more of a pity to be caught in it. Having more or less mastered the unfamiliar machine, Dan was able to drive up slowly and fairly quietly.

No lights showed in any window. Probably Guy Heron had gone back to his own bed, and he and Rose Winfrey were catching up on their sleep. This might increase or it might reduce the chance of anybody hearing the car. There was no way of predicting which, and no way of doing anything about it.

Dan wiped the steering-wheel and all the buttons on the dashboard with the tail of his ridiculous shirt. He had already wiped the tools and stowed them away. There was no reason Guy Heron should ever know his car had been borrowed, but it would not terribly matter if he did find out, unless he also found out who the borrower was.

Dan took Natasha to Willie Martin's Dutch barn, which was already half full of new hay. Dan took the string off one bale and spread the sweet hay for a bed. They were almost too tired to make love, but not quite.

Dan woke, as he had instructed himself to do, when the sky began to pale. Pretty soon there would be people about, and his new clothes were not for the public eye. Natasha woke slowly and with the utmost reluctance. She rubbed her knuckles in her eyes and pushed hay out of her hair with her fingers. She grinned sleepily at Dan. She was a girl who looked fine first thing in the morning, even though she was dirty and very short of sleep.

As soon as she was properly awake, Natasha burst out laughing. She was laughing at Dan's clothes; considering the events of the previous fifteen hours, Dan thought her laughter showed either a short memory or a very resilient character. He pulled together the bits of their bed. Willie Martin's cows would eat the hay just as happily for its having been slept on.

Dan decided to go home, since it was possible that the police had given up and gone away. Natasha agreed, still contrite about having got them into this mess. She said she was not very hungry, but Dan was ravenous. He thought of the smell of frying bacon, and nearly burst into tears.

They went as briskly as Natasha's caftan allowed. As the light strengthened, Dan became more and more self-conscious about his clothes. Even if he were not a fugitive from justice, he would have hidden in a ditch rather than be seen. They only hid in a ditch once, in the event, to avoid Joe Barton the milkman, whose whistling made more noise than the electric motor of his float.

They crossed a tributary stream of the river by a footbridge the fishing syndicate had built. Though they were in a hurry, Dan paused for a moment to marvel at the opulence of the vegetation on the stream, and beside it. Below the bridge there were two great islands of water crowfoot, leaves like green spread fingers, hairy bits of root like useless brushes, hundreds of fat white flowers with yellow centres. On the bank were tall spikes of betony, with minty leaves and clusters of purple flowers; Dan's mother had been brought up to believe that betony was a herb that cured almost everything, to be used as a compress on a cut or as an infusion to be drunk for a stomach-ache. To Dan's relief, she had lost faith in these traditional remedies. Higher up the bank, where the ground was drier, foamed the great creamy heads of the meadowsweet, reared up on red stalks with big spiky leaves, scenting the fresh morning air. Beyond again were armies of the purple spikes of loosestrife. Bright blue damsel dragonflies darted in their dozens among the flowers, looking for other insects to eat. A moorhen with comic white underpants puddled across the stream, and a family of coots went *gonk-gonk* at each other.

Dan wondered why anybody bothered with flower-gardens.

A mayfly, surviving into a second day of winged life after two years in the underwater mud, fluttered unhurriedly above the lily-pads. It was yellowish, with long opaque wings. Later in the day it would shed a final skin; its wings would become fragile, transparent, veined, and its body sharply black and white. Then, adult at last, it would find a mate, a smaller and darker male from the millions dancing over the banks. It would lay its thousands of eggs, and in a few hours it would be dead.

But not this one. Its life-cycle was cut off, incomplete. As Dan watched the awkward flight of the mayfly, he saw something he had almost never seen before. A dragonfly much larger than the blue damsels, a predatory giant with a long striped body and spots on its wings, hung high over the water as though pinned into the air. Moving almost too fast to see, it dive-bombed the mayfly, and grabbed it by the thicker upper part of its body. Dan imagined the dragonfly must grab its prey with its legs and with its jaws. The mayfly fluttered wildly, but it was securely held. The dragonfly was motionless again, its gauzy wings quite capable of carrying the burden of the mayfly as well as its own weight. It sped away to eat its breakfast somewhere else, as a kestrel carries the mouse it has killed into the next field.

Dan wondered if the death of the mayfly was a parable. Then, suddenly maddened by the thought of fried bacon, he hurried Natasha on.

The police were still at the cottage.

Old Mrs Mallett was quite pleased to come downstairs, step by laborious step, and find them cooking breakfast. She mouthed and screeched and whimpered at them. She was not prepared to allow them to guess that she could say anything or understand anything, or they'd want to know about little Natasha's dainty underthings. At the same time she was not prepared to let them get away without giving the dogs a run, filling the kitchen barrel from the well, and stocking up the chest with firewood. They fed the bantams and the pigeons without being told.

After breakfast, old Mrs Mallett became impatient. She had enjoyed her play-acting, but the party had gone on long enough. Visitors who outstayed their welcome were like fish: they began to stink. Mrs Mallett conveyed by whines and grumbles that she wanted the policemen out of the house.

They went, but only a little way. They hid themselves in the wood behind the cottage. Old Mrs Mallett heard them crashing and crunching in the undergrowth, not being in the way of prowling and creeping. They were hoping to ambush Dan and little Natasha. A fat chance they had. Natasha would look after Dan.

A night they had spent together, those two runagates. Heaven knew where. It was another bond. Dan was getting tied up tighter and tighter, to the daughter of a chartered accountant with a five-bedroom house in a nice suburb. Mrs Mallett sighed happily, drinking her fourth cup of tea that looked like liquid chocolate. Her dreams were coming true. All that remained was to sort out this bothersome business of murders. They could get on with that as soon as the police were out of the way and the family reassembled.

Mrs Mallett hoped the children would have Natasha's hair and Dan's eyes.

Dan left Natasha deep in the Priory Woods and scouted ahead by himself. Exactly as though he were planning to snare a pheasant, or avoid a watchdog, or burgle a house, he put himself in the place of the other side. Cutting short what was probably a long and tortuous mental process, that meant that the bluebottles would be lurking in the wood near the cottage. It was something they were just plain bound to do. At least, it was something Dan had to assume they'd do. They'd be failing in their duty if they didn't squat among the brambles, waiting for him. On all past form, one of the occupying bobbies would be the detective-sergeant with the face like a Hereford bullock – nothing would keep *him* away from a chance to nab the notorious Beast of Medwell Fratrorum – and he was not a bloke to fail in his duty.

Dan went very carefully, using his intimate knowledge of the uneven ground and the varieties of undergrowth. He was below ground level much of the time, using drains and ditches and rabbit-workings. He was glad it was a fine dry summer; other crawls at other moments of crisis had put him in mind of public exhibitions he had read of, in Hamburg or some such place, where women wrestled in several inches of mud. He tried to be careful of his fine new beachwear; he was not fond of his present garments but they were the only ones he had.

He saw one policeman. There would be more than one. After a painstaking circuit he spotted the other. They were near enough to communicate, but far enough apart to see, between them, three sides of the cottage. There might be a third policeman watching the front, but Dan thought not. They were putting themselves in his shoes, as he had put himself in theirs; they were making the assumption that he wouldn't go boldly up to the front door, not a sneaky villain like him, not when he was on the run.

Dan found that a plan had made itself in his head. He was not sure it was a very good plan, but he was becoming too hungry to think clearly.

He started to crawl back to Natasha.

When he reached the place where he had left her, he saw with surprise that she was standing up, with her back to him. He had expected her to be sitting or lying down: perhaps to have gone back to sleep. But she was peering at the bark of a tree, at some small bug which was eating or nesting or exuding froth. Dan had infected her, it seemed, with some of his own life-long fascination with the doings of the creatures about them who lived their lives so much more sensibly than humans did. Dan was pleased. It seemed crazy to be put down in the middle of a fascinating world and not take an interest in it.

Standing up in her bold beach caftan, Natasha was quite safe. The police were a long way away and looking in the wrong direction.

Natasha's long fair hair, wildly unkempt, fell down her back outside the caftan. From behind, the caftan had the look of a dressing-gown. It was the first time Dan had seen Natasha in such a garment, and it made her look like somebody else. A thought buzzed at the edge of Dan's mind, elusive as a gnat. He tried to grab it, but it buzzed away as fast as the murderous dragonfly. It seemed to Dan that, if he could catch the thought and examine it, he would find it was important. It was annoying to be so sleepy and so hungry. The thought danced away, mocking. It would return, if it did, unbidden and unchased, but not before Dan had had his breakfast.

Natasha turned; she smiled when she saw Dan. It was a smile of amusement at his clothes and of pleasure at seeing him. Smiling, she looked like nobody else except herself. Dan felt a wave of affection for this gallant, trusting and resourceful girl, which was all the sweeter because he knew it was returned.

Dan's plan was not original. It was derived from flickering memories of an English film comedy – one of those to which, in the days of his being better dressed than he was now, he had taken the sisters of his colleagues in the bank to the Milchester Odeon. Most of those films had been, for him, simply the necessary preliminaries to indecorous nights. But lessons could sometimes be learned. Technique For Distracting Police Who Were Watching Cottage: other occasions had produced other methods, but that old Ealing comedy one was the best for today.

There was, as often on brilliant midsummer days, a gusty wind blowing from the north-east. The wind was necessary and the direction helpful. The whole thing would cost a bit of money, but if it worked it would be money well spent.

Dan explained his plan to Natasha. She said it was so ridiculous it would probably work. This being precisely Dan's view, they got on with it.

The first stop was the rabbit-hole where Dan kept his current account. He never touched that other and much deeper hole which housed his deposit account, except to add to it. Under Natasha's astonished eyes, Dan disinterred a bundle of pound notes. Reluctantly, and after thought, he enriched the mixture with a few fivers. He put the money down the front of his shirt, because his ludicrous resort trousers had no pockets.

He led Natasha a long way round, so that they approached the cottage and the lurking police from the north-east. They were now directly upwind of the police; had the police been deer, they would have sniffed the scent of the newcomers coming downwind and scampered off through the trees. Sound would also travel downwind, and the police had ears if not noses. The wind was making a fair amount of noise in the trees, but Dan moved very quietly, and embarked on the next stage carefully.

He built a small bonfire.

He collected a little pile of dead leaves, fallen the previous autumn and now dried to crackling tinder by the midsummer sun. On the leaves he arranged a wigwam of dry twigs. Beside the wigwam he put ready a pile of larger sticks, making sure that each one was dead and dry. Then, from places that were soggy even in the longest spell of hot dry weather, he collected another pile of crumbling, spongy wood, damp to the touch and pungent with decay. He felt for the matches in his pockets. He remembered that he had neither pockets nor matches. He swore softly.

'Brain softened by hunger,' he murmured.

'Rub two sticks together,' suggested Natasha.

'Not as easy as it sounds. Noisy, too. No, it means a crawl to my safe-deposit box.'

'Is that another rabbit-hole?'

'That sort of thing. Will you wait here? Watch out for the bluebottles. They just might come stumping round.'

'Why do we want a fire?'

'Diversions. Excitement of the chase. I got the idea from Stanley Holloway, I think.'

After another long crawl, which made too much crawling altogether, Dan reached the hole where he stored pieces of silver and other *objets de vertu*, safe in polythene sacks, against the time of their sale to the bent antique shop in Milchester. Clanking and rustling as little as possible, he found the silver 'Georgian' table-lighter which he had acquired almost by accident, or instinct, from the sideboard in the Old Mill, where Mr and Mrs Potter thought spending money meant living graciously.

He snapped the lighter. There was a good spark, but no fuel. The spark would have to do.

Once again he crawled, taking no less trouble. It would have been silly to jeopardize the plan by being spotted now. He went so quietly that he surprised Natasha, who almost let out a squeak. She had not seen or heard anything. It could be assumed, with almost perfect confidence, that the policemen had not moved. The wind still gusted from the same quarter.

After a long time, punctuated by the interminable clicking of the lighter, Dan contrived to get a single dry leaf glowing. He put it with other dry leaves, and blew first gently and then more powerfully. A baby flame sprang to life among the leaves. Dan blew. The flame spread. The dry twigs crackled, perhaps just audible at a short distance over the noise of the wind in the branches. Dan added his larger sticks. The flames were pale in the bright sunshine in the little clearing Dan had chosen for his boy-scouting. Because of the slight rise and fall in the ground, the fire would not be visible to anybody on the other side of the track unless it were a lot bigger. The dry sticks and leaves made very little smoke. What smoke there was went straight towards the hidden policemen. Soon they would smell the fire. Dan began to add the damp, decomposing lumps of wood he had collected. It hissed and smoked, and dozens of woodlice ran out of the crannies. Dan began to add pound notes and five-pound notes which he pulled from the front of his shirt. Natasha did squeak, with dismay at seeing the money burn. As soon as the notes caught, nearly all of them flew upwards and away on the ever-denser smoke of the wet wood.

Dan dumped the rest of the money on top of his fire. It was no time to stint a few quid. There was a shout. One policeman was telling his mate that burning currency was falling from heaven.

'Time we got away out of this,' murmured Dan.

He led Natasha, crawling, away from the fire and into the depth of the wood. Making a slight circuit, he approached the cottage. They lay in thick undergrowth, watching the front door of the cottage and the track beyond. One of the policeman burst out of cover, and began crashing towards the source of burning wealth.

'The other must go too,' murmured Dan. 'Human nature. At least, I think so.'

He was right. In a moment both policemen could be heard kicking out the fire in order to rescue the remaining notes.

Dan jumped to his feet, and sped to his own front door. He opened it. Hidden by the half-open door, he beckoned urgently to Natasha. She followed him across the patch of open ground where Dan's mother had once grown cabbages and sweet peas. Dan shut the door behind her.

'Wherever did ye come by 'ose breeches?' said Dan's mother. 'We ben haven policemen like other folks ben haven mice.'

'They'll know that was you,' said Natasha to Dan. 'They'll come and find us in a minute.'

'Me burn good money?' said Dan. 'They'll think it was a kid with his Dad's matches, too young to know the value of that green stuff. Or a loony. A tramp drinking meths an' getting muddled. Not Mallett the rapacious bandit. Let's have the pan on the heat, and let's have some normal clothes.'

The police had left a note for Dan. It invited him to report urgently to the Medwell police station, where he was required for questioning about certain episodes. He was not suspected of any felony at this time, and there was no warrant out for his arrest. Miss Chapman, if available, was also urgently wanted. She would be quite free to leave as soon as certain confidential information had been given to her.

'It's a trap,' said Natasha immediately.

'I think it must be,' said Dan. 'Confidential information? Free to leave? No warrant?'

'A-knew it ben a trap soon's A-saw un,' said old Mrs Mallett.

'Would they do that?' said Natasha. 'Tell those fibs to trap us?'

'Jim Gundry's up to any mischief,' said Dan. 'Specially to nab me.'

'Sneaken villain,' said old Mrs Mallett.

Three-quarters of an hour later, Dan found that bacon and eggs and coffee had restored the proper working of his brain. He glanced at Natasha, standing with her back to him at the sink. Her back view, small and long-haired, had earlier in the morning put a thought into his head which he knew was important but which he could not identify. He identified it now. From behind, from a distance, Natasha looked very like Rose Winfrey.

Sharron Syme really had seen a small female figure at Lady Dodds-Freeman's door on the night of the first murder after all.

It was Rose Winfrey. Her colourless hair had looked yellow in the light from her own bedroom window. Mrs Winfrey had gone into the flat, or had seen into it without going in. She had seen the murder committed, or just about to be committed, or just having been committed. Then she had got her husband to blackmail the murderer, probably making him say that it was he, not she, who could identify the murderer. In that way she had got him killed, though in fairness Dan supposed she had not expected or intended such a result.

Dan's mother was talking. Natasha was talking. But Dan was too full of his discovery to take any of it in.

Sharron Syme might have been persuaded to change her story from truth to falsehood, or rather from expressed certainty to expressed doubt, by being offered enough money. Yes, that was credible; that was the old Sharron.

Aidan Winfrey had done what his wife told him to do, because he had always had to do what his wife told him to do, because she was the one with the money. Obviously some of the blackmail money paid by the murderer had gone to Sharron. Why had it? If she was telling the truth, why pay her anything? To buy her silence about their affair? Or because she had not told the police the whole truth? Maybe she had seen that the female at Lady Dodds-Freeman's door was middle-aged, not a girl. Maybe she had so sufficiently described the woman to Aidan Winfrey that he knew it was his wife she was talking about. *That* would be something to pay Sharron to keep quiet about. Maybe Aidan Winfrey thought his wife was actually the murderer. Maybe she *was* the murderer. Maybe Aidan Winfrey was blackmailing his wife, and Sharron knew about it and was blackmailing Aidan Winfrey . . .

Too many maybes. A horrible swarm of maybes, which seemed to grow and grow with time, like greenfly on a rose-bush.

Dan passed on his revelation, and all attendant maybes, to his superior officers.

"I don't look the least like that woman from behind,' said Natasha indignantly. 'She must weigh at least two stone more than I do.'

'Sharron didn't take measurements,' said Dan.

'I should think not, indeed,' said Dan's mother. 'Fine doens, runnen up t'strangers wi' a tape-measure.'

Dan's mother commanded Dan to find out, without further delay, mucking about or incompetence, who had killed Mrs Addison and Mr Winfrey, so that Natasha could take her rightful place in the world instead of being hunted from pillar to post by a lot of policemen. Dan meekly accepted this order. But he was further than ever from having any idea how to do it.

In the middle of the morning a police car stopped in the track near the cottage. Old Mrs Mallett woke Dan and Natasha, who were heavily asleep after their heavy breakfast. Dan squinted out of an upstairs window, he and Natasha ready to go down the apple-tree. The two lurking policemen, enriched by an uncertain number of charred banknotes, came out of the hiding-places to which they had uselessly returned. They went off in the car. The siege was lifted. They'd either given up hope or had thought of something better to do, like finding the actual murderer.

Dan decided to go to the Monk's House yet again, because he could think of nothing else to do, and because it was there, if anywhere, that he might stumble on something useful. As he went out, he paused in the door and glanced back. Natasha and his mother were sitting at the table, deep in talk about – of all extraordinary topics – Natasha's home life in Surbiton. They looked like a Victorian painting called 'Confidences' or 'Age Instructing Youth'. Dan marvelled. He was still amazed at his mother's acceptance of Natasha – her besottedness, it seemed, with Natasha.

There was no sign of life at the Monk's House. Lady Dodds-Freeman's curtains were all closed over the big windows: either she was still sleeping peacefully after last night's gin, or she was sleeping peacefully after this morning's gin. Rose Winfrey's curtains were half drawn. That might mean anything, and probably meant nothing. Dan prowled round, keeping out of sight. Guy Heron's car had gone. He was out shopping, or out for the day, or back in London at his strange job. If Dan had left any fingerprints in the car, Guy Heron would by now have covered them up. Probably he would not have noticed that the petrol was a little lower, because it was only a little lower.

Mrs Heron came out of her flat, wearing a big hat and a gardening apron. She began hammering a post into the ground, intending, no doubt, to grow something up it. Perhaps it was to be a gracious floral memorial to her late sister, a clematis or a climbing rose. Dan wondered if anybody would plant anything when he himself died. Idly he wondered what flower would be suitable. Eyebright? Pimpernel? Love-in-Idleness? From the middle of a laurel hedge he watched Mrs Heron, his mind elsewhere.

Rose Winfrey, visible for a moment in the sunlight, drew her curtains fully open. Her day began late because her nights were so tiring.

One of Lady Dodds-Freeman's curtains twitched. Perhaps she was trying to open it, but had forgotten how. Dan repressed a desire to go and help the poor old thing. Seeing him would mean nothing to her, but his being seen by anybody else would be a bad idea.

Suddenly, and as certainly as though he had been there, Dan knew what had happened.

10

Dan sat back on his heels, in the middle of the laurels, stupefied by the revelation he had just been vouchsafed. He was less comfortable, but also less visible and much less audible, than the noisy starlings and sparrows with whom he shared the laurels. His discomfort was not so much physical as mental. He was as upset by the truth he now faced as he had been by the suspicion, short-lived but at the time unavoidable, that Natasha had committed the first murder.

It was more than ever obvious that the murder of Mrs Addison had been unpremeditated, unintended, the identity of the rash intruder probably unknown to the thief until the gin-bottle had done its work. The second murder was another matter: Aidan Winfrey's death had been the planned and cold-blooded elimination of a nuisance. You could almost feel sorry for the murderer, first time round. Not second time round. That was a nasty one, and somehow the rain of that night made it worse.

Old Lizzie Bunn came out of Rose Winfrey's flat, where she went most days to do the cleaning. She saw Mrs Heron in her part of the garden and went across to talk to her. She would have gone across to talk to a statue, since she was not interested in hearing news or opinion but only in providing them. Mrs Heron had an air of standing it as long as she could; then she went into her own flat, leaving Lizzie Bunn talking to the roses. This palled; Lizzie rode away crossly on her smart new bicycle.

The curtain which had twitched in Lady Dodds-Freeman's flat was now opened six inches. No more. The old lady had either decided that was enough or had exhausted herself with the six inches, a further effort, perhaps, to be made later, or the morning spent in kindly gloom among the bottles.

That was the limit of the action Dan could observe; that was the life of the Monk's House.

Absently, absorbed in his thoughts, he watched more purposeful action going on between his feet. There was a little round hole in the ground, at the edge of the laurels. An insect buzzed up, carrying a small green disc, and disappeared into the hole, dragging the disc with it. It was a leaf-cutter bee that had cut the disc from a rose leaf, leaving a circular hole, and was using the bit of leaf to line its house. Her house – the females did all the work. She would have half a dozen cells, each lined with little discs of rose-leaf and each then filled with pollen. She would lay an egg in each of the cells and then seal them up like somebody preserving greengages. She would give each baby bee just the right amount of pollen for its growth, and in the spring, full grown, it would bite its way out and either be a drone or another busy housewife.

It was all in sharp contrast to the lifestyle of the Monk's House, where the women were drones as well as housewives, and where the amount of provisions was wastefully lavish. But it was true that none of the ladies defaced rose bushes by cutting little round holes in their leaves.

Mrs Heron could be seen peeping out of an upstairs window. She was making sure Lizzie Bunn had taken herself off. Mrs Heron, by all accounts, gave her baby an awful lot of pollen, but presumably no more than he thought he needed, or she thought he needed. She came out of the house and resumed her gardening.

Dan wondered how to expose the murderer without getting anybody else killed. The obvious approach was by another apparent blackmail attempt, this goading the murderer into trying to kill the apparent blackmailer and the attempt being, with any luck, prevented. There were problems of casting and of communication. It would all have to be very much better managed than on the night of the thunderstorm, which Dan realized now had been distinctly slapdash.

The thing was to make use of the weaknesses of the quarry, its habits or preoccupations. Pheasants, for example, had a habit of always going the same way when they went out of their covert in the early morning to feed; and if they were only going a short distance they preferred walking to flying, unless somebody was chasing them or shooting at them, and sometimes even then. It was on the basis of these two things that you placed your snares. In this present case the weakness, if you could call it that, was equally obvious, and showed the right angle of approach.

But there was a bit of groundwork to do first. Dan wanted a telephone. He wondered about using Lady Dodds-Freeman's again, but it was still early in the day, and the old thing might be making pretty good sense. Rose Winfrey was in her flat. Mrs Heron was out of hers, and young Mr Guy Heron had gone off in his car. Mrs Heron was far enough away from her own telephone not to hear somebody using it, unless they bellowed, and Dan had no intention of bellowing. It was a question of whether, while he was telephoning, he could see out into Mrs Heron's garden; it depended where her telephone was, and how long a flex it had.

He imagined her back door would be unlocked, in the middle of the morning in this quiet place, and that he could get to it unobserved. It was, and he could.

Dan went in. He glanced round, from force of semi-professional habit, to what there was that had a high value-bulk ratio. The pictures looked the work of a conscientious amateur; the clocks were just clocks from a shop; there was no silver on display and the spoons in the sideboard were plate.

The telephone was on a little table in the window of the over-furnished sitting-room. Using it as an honest man would have used it, Dan would have been able to see Mrs Heron easily, and she would have been able to see him almost equally easily. He could have squatted and kept his hostess in view by peeping over the windowsill. But he was going to use one of his acquired voices, and the performance required a performance. He could not sound like a solicitor while squatting on an Indian rug. He put a dainty upright chair beside the telephone. He looked up the number he wanted in the local book on a shelf in the telephone-table. He dialled.

He heard the telephone ringing in Rose Winfrey's flat next door. The rings coincided with the buzzes he heard in his receiver. He made a face like a solicitor, and waited for Mrs Winfrey to answer.

She answered.

'Mrs Winfrey?' said Dan, through thin, unsmiling solicitor's lips.

'Yes.'

Dan could not hear Mrs Winfrey's actual voice through the wall dividing the flats, over the voice he was getting on the telephone. It followed that she could not hear his.

Dan said that he was George Maltravers, of Chapman and Maltravers, Solicitors, of West Hugley.

'West what?' said Mrs Winfrey.

'Hugley,' said Dan, there being no such place as West Hugley.

Dan said that, shortly before his tragic and deplorable death, the late Mr Aidan Winfrey had lodged with them a sealed letter. It was to be opened in the event of his sudden death, whether the circumstances appeared suspicious or not.

'Oh?' said Mrs Winfrey, sounding a good deal surprised.

'We were instructed to take such action as would be immediately and evidently proper, having read the information revealed in Mr Winfrey's letter.'

'Well, have you?'

'On the day following your late husband's death, this office was burgled by, as we believed, an employee who had been dismissed but who unfortunately knew the combination of the safe. We were confident of recovering the papers that had rested in the safe, since they were of no intrinsic value, though we were not confident of recovering the modest amount of petty cash which was the evident reason for the robbery. We did not think it proper, in these circumstances, to trouble the clients involved by immediately acquainting them with the fact of the temporary loss of their papers.'

Dan was being a solicitor with a guilty conscience.

'However,' said Dan, allowing a note of obsequiousness to creep into his solemn voice, 'it transpired that the burglary was committed by a professional criminal, not yet identified or apprehended, and not by the man we suspected.'

'Why are you telling me all this?'

'It becomes less and likely that we shall recover the papers. The police agree with us that it becomes more and more likely that the criminal has destroyed all of those from which no easy profit could be made.'

'So?' Rose Winfrey was not in a voluble mood. Perhaps she never was.

'So, Mrs Winfrey, being most anxious to proceed according to the late Mr Winfrey's instructions, we appeal to you.'

'For what?' She was slow, as well as taciturn. No, not really slow, in fact in some ways quite shockingly quick.

'For some idea as to the contents of the letter which Mr Winfrey lodged with us. We assume that he discussed it with you?'

'No. This is the first I've heard about any letter. I don't know what he would have said, or what he would have wanted you to do. I can't help you at all.' Dan thought she had finished, but after a pause she added, without apparent sincerity, 'I'm sorry.'

Dan apologized for troubling her. She said again that she was sorry she could not help. In a flurry of mutual apology they both rang off.

Preoccupation with his role, and with saying exactly the right thing, had made Dan forget Mrs Heron. He remembered her now. She was still there, banging another split-chestnut post into the bed beside her grass path.

He thought he heard, from the next door flat, the ping of Mrs Winfrey starting another call.

A letter left by Aidan Winfrey with a solicitor, to be opened and acted upon in the event of his sudden death: it was not improbable. The existence of the letter would protect him from being murdered, if the murderer knew about it. Perhaps, if the letter had existed, it would have protected him. Anyway, the letter now had a kind of objective existence; Rose Winfrey would believe that there had been a letter, and that it had been stolen, and that it was probably now in ashes or in some remote dustbin.

Other people would shortly be hearing about that letter. Rose Winfrey would be asked about it. Yes, she would say, there was such a letter, the lawyers rang me up about it.

Dan had another telephone call to make, but he needed

Natasha in order to make it. And it would be better to let matters proceed under their own secret momentum for an hour or two. Pleased with himself, he slipped out and away.

Natasha met him in the wood by the cottage.

'The police came back again. Two different ones. Luckily I'd washed up breakfast, so there was no way of telling we'd been there. They didn't stay long. I think they find your mother rather tiring.'

Dan laughed. They went in to cook lunch, but referred to it, to old Mrs Mallett, as dinner.

Dan asked Natasha the name of the firm Guy Heron worked for. She had forgotten. It was Something and Something, like most of the others; she had been to dozens of them to audition for television commercials. But given a telephone, she thought she could find out from a friend.

'Why do you want to know?'

'Another stratagem.'

'Better than the last one, I hope.'

'I hope so too.'

'No more murderens,' ordered old Mrs Mallett.

Natasha said she was more likely to reach her friends in the evening, for few of them were actually working on the legitimate stage. It was also better for her to cross the country in the evening, because then she could travel on the back of Dan's bicycle.

Since it was to be the evening, as good a telephone as any to use was Lady Dodds-Freeman's. She would probably be making no sense; certainly not much. She had forgotten how to bolt her back door, though her front door closed on a spring lock. The only likely hazard was PC Gundry, and Dan could keep a lookout for him while Natasha telephoned.

The old lady was a depressing sight, unkempt, raffish, wearing odd shoes, dribbling, singing to herself in front of a silent television set. The flat itself was not squalid, because PC Gundry's wife Beryl had been coming in. She was not being paid, and even the villagers of Medwell Fratrorum did not suspect her of nicking anything. Dan admitted to himself that it was good of Beryl, as it was pretty good of Jim Gundry to keep an eye on things here. It would be better if he didn't do it tonight, but it was a good thing he did it other times.

Natasha got on to a friend in London almost at once. The friend was astonished at hearing Natasha, and at hearing what she wanted. But she knew the answer. Guy Heron worked as an executive at Parker and Pochin, who had offices near Paddington Station.

They looked up Parker and Pochin in Lady Dodds-Freeman's London directory, and Dan made a note of the number.

PC Gundry did come. They heard him in the next room rousing Lady Dodds-Freeman out of her coma and starting to help her to bed. His tone was firm but jolly – about the right tone to use, Dan thought. Under cover of the jollity, and of the old lady being got to her bedroom, Dan and Natasha slipped out of the back door.

Dan confirmed that Guy Heron's car was still away. It seemed highly likely that he was back in his office, or would be the next morning. The murder of an aunt would not bring indefinite leave, especially as Mrs Heron was far from prostrate.

Dan made three attempts, on three different telephones, to talk to Guy Heron in his office. The secretary who answered the telephone thought Dan was a funny one, because he wouldn't leave a number for Mr Heron to ring back. She also found him difficult to understand. He was not using, to a London secretary, his broadest and most fanciful voice, but a kind of gravelly in-between voice. It was the gravel that made for problems in communication. When he finally got on to to Guy Heron he moderated the gravel; he wanted full comprehension at the other end.

He said, 'Not to put too fine a point on it, Mr Heron, I'm a professional criminal, a burglar. I done a lawyer's office the other night, took some cash an' a lot of letters. I just got round to readin' the letters. There's one might interest you, an' if it don't interest you it'll sure as hell interest the fuzz.'

There was a kind of croak at the other end, not of astonishment but of concern. Perhaps alarm, perhaps not. But not surprise; not puzzlement. Rose Winfrey had already told him, then, about the call from the mythical lawyer. No doubt she had the number of his London flat. Probably she had phoned in the evening, possibly just when Natasha was getting the name of his advertising agency.

The effect of this was to put beyond doubt, in Guy Heron's mind, the existence of a letter lodged by Aidan Winfrey with a lawyer. What was the letter going to say?

'What does the letter say?' asked Guy Heron.

'It says what somebody saw, a few nights ago when a lady got done in. That's what it says.'

'What does it say the person saw?'

Dan had foreseen this question, and sidestepped it. Guy Heron knew far better than he himself did what had happened in Lady Dodds-Freeman's flat. If he went into detail, he risked giving away the phoniness of the letter.

He said, 'I'll tell you better when I see you.'

'What in hell has any of this got to do with me? I was in London the night my aunt was killed.'

'Ow,' said Dan, remembering there was no reason the burglar should know about this relationship, unless he had read about the inquest in the local paper. 'Your auntie, was it? Makes it worse, that does.'

'What do you mean by that?'

Dan had no idea what he had meant. He sidestepped again. He said, 'I hopes as you're comin' down to visit your ma this weekend.'

Guy Heron was. Dan told him to stand by for further instructions, and to have a thousand pounds in cash.

Guy Heron sounded curiously unperturbed. That was because he was not a man who fought his own battles. At least, Dan assumed that was the reason.

Dan growled a few generalized threats, and hung up.

It would have been tidy, and economical of the awful effort of finding and using telephones, to give Guy Heron a rendezvous there and then. But Dan wanted the rendezvous to be fixed at the last possible minute. Also, he had not made a plan about the rendezvous. It needed a number of special characteristics, including being near Medwell, being a place Dan could get to unseen, a place Guy Heron could get his car near, a private place, and a trap. Dan was sure he would think of a place, but he had not done so yet.

Hungry after so much telephoning, Dan went home to lunch. The police had been again: been and gone without finding anything, and without saying anything to Dan's mother.

'It's persecution,' said Natasha. 'I had to spend half the morning in the wood, when I wanted to wash my hair.'

'I expect they're feeling a bit persecuted, too,' said Dan, thinking of policemen caught between the upper millstone of the Detective Chief Superintendent and the nether millstone of repeated visits to his mother.

Meanwhile Dan's telephone calls would continue to breed more telephone calls. Guy Heron would be running, figuratively, to his mother, if only out of habit. Mrs Heron would consequently know about the 'letter'. Perhaps she knew about it already, from Rose Winfrey – Dan had no means of knowing what terms those two were on. Mrs Winfrey would get confirmation from Guy Heron that her husband had written a letter.

She would assume that the letter spelled out what she herself had told her husband she had seen in Lady Dodds-Freeman's flat. All three of them would assume that the letter described what she had seen that night. No other assumption was possible. The letter might make the admission that the writer, Aidan Winfrey, was blackmailing the murderer: but, if the blackmailer was dead, he was not much harmed by that confession. His widow might be, but he might not mind much about that.

Dan found himself thinking as though there really was a letter, and speculating about its contents. He reminded himself, confused, that he must restrict himself to speculating about the others' speculations.

'But if the burglar's got the letter Aidan Winfrey left the lawyer,' said Natasha. 'Oh . . .'

Dan, too, had to remind himself again that there was no burglar, no letter and no lawyer.

'Letters,' grumbled old Mrs Mallett. 'Twenty year sen I had one o' they.'

'What's the point of the whole letter hassle?' said Natasha. 'Things were complicated enough as it was.'

'The murderer must have thought Aidan Winfrey saw him,' said Dan, speaking carefully, because he was in danger of getting into a muddle himself. 'Hence the bang in the thunderstorm. Murderer thought he was off the hook after that. Now up pops a burglar with a letter that puts the murderer right back on the hook. I know there isn't any burglar or any letter,' he added quickly, as Natasha opened her mouth to speak, 'but as long as the murderer thinks there is, he's going to have to do something about it. With either money or a blunt instrument.'

'So we have to have a stand-in burglar.'

'No. We'll surprise them. We'll have a stand-in blackmailer instead.'

'Who?'

'You.'

11

On Friday evening, from the laurels, Dan and Natasha saw young Mr Guy Heron arrive at the Monk's House in his trendy clothes and his sports car. They did not immediately seek a telephone. They waited for an hour, until Lady Dodds-Freeman would be adequately drunk. Then they went in through her back door, to the extension telephone in her bedroom.

Natasha kept watch while Dan telephoned the Herons' flat. He used his burglar voice, which entailed putting on a repulsive burglar face. He told Guy Heron that he would sell him Aidan Winfrey's letter for £1,000.

There were muffled noises from the Herons' telephone. Guy Heron was covering the mouthpiece while he conferred with his mother. A plan was being made, or would shortly be made, presumably with the object of getting the letter without spending £1,000.

Dan wished that there were a letter, and that he were the burglar who had it.

Guy Heron resumed communication. Dan told him where to be at 8 p.m. the following evening, which would give him time to raise the money, or commit suicide, or whatever he proposed.

Dan rang the police – not PC Gundry, from whom he doubted if he could conceal his voice under any grotesqueries, but the station officer in Milchester. He said he was Captain Cedric Maltravers, visiting the area from Yorkshire. In an extraordinary way, and by utter coincidence, he had come into possession of certain information. It was that the murderer of the late Mrs Gwyneth Addison and of the late Mr Aidan Winfrey would be at a certain place at eight the following evening, with the intention of either buying back an incriminating document or repossessing the document by dint of murdering its possessor. If the police were there, in hiding, villains would be unmasked and innocent persons exonerated.

The station officer sounded greatly surprised by this. He sounded suspicious and incredulous. He wanted Captain Maltravers's address, and an account of the way he had come by his information. He wanted an immediate interview with Captain Maltravers.

Dan had been expecting this reaction and was ready for it.

'Great Scott!' he shouted softly to the telephone, with a military rasp muted by fear of arousing Lady Dodds-Freeman. 'My dogs are savaging the lambs!'

'Where can I reach –?' began the station officer.

Dan hung up, with the finality of a man who sees lambs savaged by dogs. The police might think it was a hoax or worse, but they would be bound to follow up the tip. Even on a Saturday night they would not take the risk of passing up the chance, even though the chance might seem to them 100 to 1 against. At least, Dan thought not.

'Last time you were too simple,' said Natasha. 'This time you're too complicated.'

Dan once again cocooned himself in front of the kitchen fire. He was aware once again of Natasha directly above him. He longed to join her, and he thought she would like that too. But climbing the steep little stairs would make a noise like a volley of rifle shots; and his mother was a light sleeper with a suspicious mind.

It was fine to be home, but there were serious disadvantages.

There was a movement outside. Though sleepy, Dan was rendered intensely alert and suspicious by everything that had been going on. He unwrapped himself from his cocoon, and prowled to the door. He crouched, listening, in the dark kitchen.

A little voice whispered, 'It's me.'

Dan opened the door to Natasha. She had climbed out of his

bedroom window and down the old apple tree to the ground. Her shirt reached half-way down her thighs; her legs and feet were bare.

'I think the stairs creak,' she whispered.

Old Mrs Mallett once again lay listening intently for a creak on the stairs. She heard instead murmurs and rustlings from below. The slyboots had used the window, then, as Dan had done so many hundred times. Many was the leathering he had missed by using that window, and many was the leathering he'd got. Much good it had done. Natasha was better medicine.

Once again Natasha cried with joy, so that Dan had to put his hand over her mouth to keep her quiet. He even made a caress out of that.

Old Mrs Mallett, snug in her bed, heard Natasha climb the apple tree and go through the window, Dan-style. She was a bouncy one then, an active maid. That raised a doubt about the future as Mrs Mallett planned it. But not a serious doubt. The important thing about Natasha was not that she climbed up and down trees, but that her father was a chartered accountant with a five-bedroomed house in a nice London suburb.

Time was, Mrs Mallett would have been outraged by the night's goings on. In her own kitchen! But age had mellowed her ideas, in some directions. (Not in all: not in the matter of Dan's future.) It was all a means to an end. Dan was getting himself trussed up in a neat parcel with the address written clear. It was doing it at home, under her very eye, that made the big difference. If he had his wicked way with a hussy under a hedge, he could walk away from the whole thing, nobody the wiser, no strings to hold him. Now she had something to face him with – she, and pretty Natasha, and the chartered accountant in Surbiton.

Old Mrs Mallett heard a muted jangle of springs from Dan's bed, as Natasha climbed back into it. She thought she heard a long, happy, trembling sigh. She sighed herself, and was lulled into a doze by visions of golden privet.

At breakfast, Natasha's eyes were dreamy, and Dan seemed in a mood to grin. Mrs Mallett was in a mood to wink.

The domestic routine of Saturday morning in the cottage was disrupted by yet another visit from the police. They did not bother with old Mrs Mallett. They neither asked her anything nor told her anything, but left a note. They were learning. They hung about crossly for half an hour, then went away in a Volvo.

Old Mrs Mallett got herself across the kitchen, found her spectacles, and read the note, quickly, before Dan and Natasha came back.

It was another urgent request for them both to go to the police station.

Mrs Mallett scrumpled it up and dropped it into the kitchen fire.

Probably it was another trap, and the young were that silly and trusting they might just fall for it. Just possibly it was not a trap at all but meant what it said. If Natasha were free to go, go she would, sooner or later, and maybe sooner rather than later. That was no part of old Mrs Mallett's plan. Natasha was to stay in the cottage a sight more days and, more by token, a sight more nights. So the fire was the place for the policemen's note.

'Let me get this quite clear,' said Natasha. 'I don't think I will, actually, but let me try. You now think Guy Heron was told by his mother about the existence of that money. He jumped into his car and came down here. While he was taking the money he bashed his aunt, probably not knowing until afterwards who she was. But Rose Winfrey saw him through the window, and told her husband. He started blackmailing Guy Heron, who therefore shot him, with his own gun that he'd pretended was stolen. Now *we're* pretending a burglar is blackmailing Guy

Heron, and I'm supposed to imitate Rose Winfrey, because you've got an absurd idea I look like her –'

'Only from behind,' said Dan apologetically. 'Fleeting resemblance.'

'So Guy Heron is going to try to murder me, and you're going to try to stop him.'

'Assistance of the police,' said Dan. 'Long strong arm of the law.'

'Suppose they don't come? Suppose they didn't believe in your ridiculous Captain What's-his-name?'

'They'd never risk not coming. At least, I hope not.'

'So do I,' said Natasha.

'You've got it nearly right,' said Dan. 'Except for who's going to shoot at you.'

'Guy Heron.'

'No. His mother.'

'She's doing his dirty work for him?'

'No. Her own. He may be an accessory, but he's not the murderer. Would you like me to tell you exactly what happened that night?'

'Well, I can see you think you know.'

'I know, all right. This time I do know. Mrs Addison talks to her sister Mrs Heron on the telephone. The old lady's plastered and there's £5,000 lying around in heaps: that's the hot news from the old home. Mrs Heron needs that money badly, to pay her ewe-lamb's gambling debts, or something. Maybe just to contribute her share of the housekeeping. So she gets herself down here from London, arriving a bit before eleven. Easy, if Mrs Addison telephoned about six. Mrs Heron has a key to the old girl's front door. Maybe she'd had it for months. Likely the Dodds-Freemans gave their neighbours a key when they all first arrived, and the old girl forgot about it. Or maybe she picked up the key the cleaning woman left on the kitchen table. Anyway, she goes in, makes sure that Lady Dodds-Freeman's unconscious, and begins scooping up twenty-pound notes. She knocks over a little table in the dark. Crash. Picture-frames and flower-vases all over the place. Mrs Addison wakes up, Rose Winfrey wakes up. Mrs Addison, being a good neighbour, runs down, tries the door, finds it unlocked, goes in. Pretty brave, actually. Sees a dark figure up to no good. Challenges. Dark figure picks up the nearest blunt instrument to hand, which in that flat is naturally a gin-bottle. Bash. Then, and only then, she realizes who she's bashed. Rose Winfrey meanwhile has turned on her bedroom light and run downstairs and outside, which nobody thought she was capable of doing. Maybe puts on a pair of trousers, maybe wearing pyjamas. Looks in at the door. Sees exactly what's happened. Is seen, at that moment, by Sharron Syme, who's being picked up by Aidan Winfrey in his car and taken off to naughties. Aidan, of course, is thought by Rose to be in London. The rest is obvious.'

After a long pause, Natasha said, 'How awful to kill your own sister by mistake.'

'Yes. She didn't kill by mistake, but the victim was a mistake. I wonder what she would have done if she'd known it was her sister interrupting her.'

'Perhaps the same. In panic.'

'Yes, perhaps.'

'How do you know all this, Dan?'

'I watched Mrs Heron bashing chestnut posts into the ground with a sledgehammer. Doing it like a man, accurate and powerful. And the whole thing fell into place. It must have happened like I said. See how it all fits. Rose Winfrey immediately starts blackmailing Mrs Heron, using poor Aidan as her agent. So the money goes through his hands, and some of it sticks there, and some of that goes to Sharron Syme. The night he got himself killed, I guess he was blackmailing her on his own account, in order to pay off Sharron. Only Mrs Heron wasn't having any: that's why there was no money on the body. So I s'pose he'd threatened her, and then he'd gone off to meet Sharron at the summerhouse and tell her to find £500 somewhere else. Mrs Heron shot him with her son's gun, which she'd had all the time. That part of it's so infinitely more likely than that somebody pinched the gun nine months before and suddenly found a use for it. And in a funny way it's less suspicious: who'd kill a bloke with their own son's shotgun, and leave it beside the body?'

'Yes . . . the last part's convincing. But I jib at a sister bashing her sister to death with a bottle.'

'Maybe, as you said, she's have done the same anyway, in panic, in sudden desperation, even if she'd known who she was hitting. They did have rows. They got on each others' nerves. I saw them once very near losing their tempers with each other, and that was when I was there. But I don't think any of that is relevant. I'm nearly certain she just hit out in panic, and then realized what she'd done.'

'She cooled down pretty quickly. She wiped the fingerprints off the bottle, and she took all the money back to bed with her.'

'It'd be silly to leave it behind, wouldn't it, after taking all that trouble to get it.'

'Does Guy know about all this?'

'I think he must know. I should think he drove down here that night, and they gave one another their alibis. I should think he's had some of the money. I should think, from what I've seen, that he's had all the money that didn't go to the Winfreys and Sharron Syme.'

'If only that old lady hadn't got drunk, none of this would have happened.'

'Moral in that,' said Dan.

They heard a car approaching. Natasha, by now as used to the routine as Dan, was half-way out of the kitchen window when she realized she was climbing into the outstretched arms of a big man. It was the detective-sergeant with the face like a Hereford bullock.

In the door, at the same moment, stood a uniformed policeman.

They had been cleverer than Dan. Dan had been monumentally stupid. They had come quietly up on foot, covering front and back; then their mates had approached noisily in a car.

Dan felt a wave of despair: some for himself, more for his mother, most for Natasha. He had let himself get cocky. His overconfidence had destroyed them all. He had simply assumed that because the police always had come up to the door in their car, they always would. Lovely elaborate sophisticated stratagems, brilliant impersonations on the telephone, a masterly web of misunderstanding and menace, plenty of fatuous patting of himself on the back: and he'd let them all be caught by a couple of country policemen who did it by walking a couple of hundred yards instead of sitting in a car.

Dan sat down on the wobbly chair, suddenly exhausted by misery.

'Didn't you get my note, ruddy Mallett?' said the sergeant through the open window. He was still embracing Natasha as though he loved her.

'Seems a-did see one note,' admitted Dan. 'A-bent rightly unnerstanden un.'

'It was a trap, wasn't it?' said Natasha, now on the ground beside the sergeant, and looking like a lamb beside a bullock.

'Trap? Trap? Course it wasn't no trap. All we wanted to do was tell you nobody wasn't lookin' for you. We tell you, in the note. Both notes. What d'you mean, trap? We don't set traps for the likes of you, Miss, only for murderers an' such. When you didn't come after we lef' the first note, we lef' another. Made sure you'd believe that un. Spelled it out, we did, so even you'd know it was genuine.'

'Never saw 'at,' said Dan.

'Gammon,' said the Sergeant.

'It's true,' said Natasha. 'We never saw a second note.'

'Then what became of 'e?' said the Sergeant.

Dan and Natasha, at the same moment, turned to look at old Mrs Mallett. She avoided their eyes, and crooned to herself like a senile songbird.

'My God, you've give us a sight o' trouble, you Mallett,' said the sergeant. 'We bin tryin' since God was a boy to get that message to you, that nobody wasn't lookin' for you.'

'Hum?' said Dan.

'Why did you think we was callin' here every day?'

'Were ye?' said Dan, taking refuge in oafishness.

'As far as Miss Chapman were concerned, after that photographer Laurence Catchpole were tragically killed by Medwell Church, as a matter o' routine we instituted inquiries. Established 'is bookin' at the Wessex Motor Inn. Established 'is delivery of a lot of photos to Padstow's Brewery. Established those photos were maybe eight hours' work.' The sergeant glanced at Natasha. 'Very nice too, Miss.'

Natasha blushed vividly.

'Established,' said the sergeant, 'from bits o' background in the photos, no doubt to be trimmed off when they was printed, that they was taken in Chalet Number Six at the motel, same like the one Mr Catchpole occupied. Which he did the night Mrs Addison was murdered. We been tryin' to tell you all this for days.'

'I'd lief see they photies,' said Dan.

'No you wouldn't,' said Natasha, blushing again, or still blushing.

'No you wouldn't,' said the sergeant severely to Dan. 'Only for grown-ups.'

'Oh,' said Dan.

'An' as for you, bleedin' Mallett, beggin' your pardon Miss, Major Coxen made a statement in strict confidence to the Super.'

'Gum,' said Dan.

'Pity your Ma can't hear or speak, or we could ha' left a message with her. Was it by any chance you burgled a property known as Woodbines, residence of Mr Edwin Colloway?'

'Never did sech,' said Dan anxiously, remembering the havoc they had left.

'Herm,' said the sergeant, sounding as well as looking like a bullock. 'Clothes we found weren't traceable, an' Mrs Calloway 'ad washed up an' put away the plates afore we got there, an' your fingerprints was near enough explained 'cos you sometimes go through the motions o' workin' there. Pity. Why was their curtains recovered in East Street, Milchester?'

'Bafflen,' said Dan.

'Herm. You know anything about a burglar wi' a letter he pinched?'

Dan looked blank.

'Or a Capting wi' a silly voice from Yorkshire?'

Dan tried to look not only blank but moronic.

'One thing we kep' quiet about,' said the sergeant. 'A lot o' the money them blokes from Brighton gave her ladyship, it were numbered. Dealin' considerable in cash transactions, they keep a big float, an' they writes wi' a felt pen on the top note of a wad how much the wad is. Normal proceedin', some like second-hand car-dealers. Confidential, we circulated a lot o' shops an' pubs wi' the numbers the Brighton blokes give us. Started pickin' 'em up immediate. All the same source, seeminly. Got un red-handed, passin' a numbered note in a butcher's. Searched the domicile, an' found most o' the rest o' the money. Routine police work, took inside of a week. Arrest was day before yesterday.'

'Who?'

'Name o' Dorothy Sawyer. Used to clean her ladyship's flat. Walked out one day an' took her latchkey with her, falsely statin' she left it behind. Her story is, she heard about the money an' all, same like the rest o' the village, an' went round to see the old lady was all right. Found the door unlocked an' the place bein robbed. Tackled the intruder, like a good citizen, an' in the resultant frackass some'ow struck the intruder on the nut wi' a bottle. Then give way to temptation, an' took the money. Says her ladyship owed her a packet o' back wages, which, her ladyship bein' a mite confused in mind, is half-way possible. So her plea's liable to be recovery of debt in regard to the money, and self-defence in regard to the homicide. Load o' rubbish, o' course. Can't see no jury swallowin' that.'

'Hum,' said Dan, feeling as stupid as he was trying to look.

'Leave catchin' murderers to us, Dan Mallet, an' go back to nickin' pheasants.'

''At Mrs Sawyer,' said Dan slowly. 'She ben an' done in 'at Mr Winfrey, too?'

'That's the presumption, as of now,' said the sergeant. 'Bein' a thievin' old bat by nature, she likely pinched Mr Heron's gun out o' his car. Prob'ly intendin' to sell it, but found that wasn't so easy. Puzzlin' detail o' some burglar tryin' to blackmail Mr Heron.' The sergeant looked hard at Dan. ''Course Mr Heron approached us immediate. 'Cos however could *he* be blackmailed?'

'Dunno,' said Dan.

'Seein' he was in the company of his managing director at a conference in London from five o'clock until midnight, the night his auntie was murdered.'

'Um,' said Dan.

'Same like his Mum were at a dinner party wi' seven reliable witnesses, from eight o'clock until midnight.'

'Ah,' said Dan.

'You an' your trap,' said the sergeant, in a tone of tolerant derision. 'Burglars an' lawyers an' such, an' letters what never existed. You made a right berk o' yourself, Dan Mallett.'

Dan was aware of pitying smiles from the policeman in the doorway, from two other policemen who were now standing behind him, from his mother; and then, after a moment, from Natasha.

Dan was feeling not only stupid and humiliated, but also cheated. Art demanded that the murderer be someone intimately connected with the Monk's House. It had always been objectively possible that a complete outsider had done it, but that was an inartistic conclusion. Dorothy Sawyer was not a complete outsider, exactly, but she was a bit player in the drama.

Of course Rose Winfrey had recognized Mrs Sawyer, who had worked all those months for Lady Dodds-Freeman. It would have been easy for the Winfreys to find out where she lived, if they did not already know. Aidan Winfrey could have blackmailed a village cleaning woman as well as a nob. And the worm would have turned just the same.

It was all grossly unsatisfactory.

Of course it was nice that he and Natasha were not going to prison.

12

'It's impossible,' murmured Dan into Natasha's cheek, in front of the kitchen fire, at one in the morning. 'I can believe old Dorothy Sawyer crept round to the Monk's House with the key she pinched, started picking up the money, got surprised by Mrs Addison, and bashed her. I can believe all that.'

'You'd better,' said Natasha sleepily. 'It's what happened.'

'Yes, but not that she shot Aidan Winfrey. I can't believe that bit. There's a dozen reasons it's impossible. People like Dorothy Sawyer don't kill people with shotguns, it's clean out of character. They bash them with gin-bottles, that's what *they* do. The gun is impossible.'

'Why?'

'I don't know why. It just is. And how could she possibly know he was going to meet somebody in the summerhouse?'

'He told her. Because he wanted another £500.'

'It's not credible. It makes no sense.'

'You're just trying to salve your pride.'

'I am trying to arrive at the truth,' said Dan with dignity.

'Forget it for now.'

Dan forgot it for now.

There was a message for Natasha, at her cousin's house in the village. A major provincial repertory company, with Equity cards in its gift, was auditioning for the autumn season. Natasha's application had been noted, and she was expected.

She was excited. She rehearsed her audition pieces, and practised her songs and her dance-routines and her tumbling.

Dan was excited for her, but he felt the cold breath of impending farewells.

Old Mrs Mallett was incensed at this development. She

dismissed Natasha's theatrical ambitions with as much energy as she cherished her own banking ambitions for Dan. She tried to cajole and then to bully Natasha into staying quietly with them in the cottage, instead of traipsing half across the country to make an exhibition of herself. She resorted to moral blackmail of the crudest kind, saying in a tiny, quavering voice that she would not last many days without Natasha to look after her.

'I'm one of 600 girls after two jobs,' said Natasha. 'I'll be back.'

Dan did not know whether to hope for Natasha's success or failure.

Obstinately, Dan continued to refuse to believe that Dorothy Sawyer had killed Aidan Winfrey with a gun. His mother and Natasha mocked him, saying he was cross because he had been proved completely wrong, that he had made a fool of himself, that there was egg all over his face, that he was not facing facts because they conflicted with his theories. Natasha expressed herself in these terms; old Mrs Mallett projected the same message in different terms.

Dan based his disbelief on simple, lifelong observation. A greenfinch built a deep, woven, cup-shaped nest in the thickest part of a hedge. A titmouse found a hole in a tree, or a knot-hole in the weatherboards of a building. It was inconceivable that a greenfinch would nest in a hole, or a titmouse build a nest in a hedge. It was as impossible as the rising of the sun in the west, or Dan's mother giving up her plans for him, or himself going along with those plans. He thought the analogy with Dorothy Sawyer was exact; he even used those pompous remembered words to himself.

That being so, who had killed Aidan Winfrey, and why?

It must have been someone Aidan Winfrey was blackmailing: that remained clear. Someone he was blackmailing as a result of what Rose Winfrey had seen, the night Mrs Addison was killed. That also remained clear. What could Rose Winfrey have seen that would have made somebody else the Winfreys' blackmail victim? Rose Winfrey wasn't going to tell. She wasn't going to admit having been anywhere near the old lady's flat. She wasn't going to admit being physically capable of getting downstairs without help. She wasn't going to admit even to having been awake as late as 11 p.m. Because, of course, she wasn't going to admit having been an accessory to blackmail.

Someone else must have been in the flat besides the drunken old lady and the victim, Mrs Addison, and the murderer, Dorothy Sawyer. An accomplice of Dorothy Sawyer's? Probably a man – shooting Aidan Winfrey to stop his demands seemed like a male thing to do. A woman like Mrs Heron was certainly capable of handling a shotgun and shooting somebody with it, but there was no way in which she could have been blackmailed.

A man, known to Rose Winfrey. Yes, he had to be known to her, but he also had to be the accomplice of Dorothy Sawyer. What kind of man could that be? The two necessary qualifications were almost totally contradictory. Nobody Rose Winfrey knew could be Dorothy Sawyer's trusted and intimate pal, but you would not take anybody other than a trusted and intimate pal on such an expedition. How about a local tradesman who delivered to the Monk's House flats? Or an electrician, a plumber, a painter? Dan ran his mental eye down the list of tradesmen who delivered in Medwell Fratrorum. Paperboy, milkman, grocer. Dan knew them, and the idea of any of them joining Dorothy Sawyer in a burglary was like a greenfinch building in a chimney. The butcher and the fishmonger from Milchester? They both had vans that came to Medwell once a week, delivering to the nobs orders made by telephone. Obviously Mrs Winfrey knew the men who came in the vans, but how could Dorothy Sawyer know them? She might happen to know one or other. It was awfully thin. There was a wine-merchant, too, who came in a Volvo estate, with cases of Beaujolais in the back. Dan had seen him but never spoken to him. It was inconceivable that Dorothy Sawyer was his intimate friend, though when she worked for Lady Dodds-Freeman she had probably met him.

A man, then, not at the time necessarily known to Mrs Winfrey, but someone she could afterwards describe and so identify? Objectively that was possible. It had the depressing effect, once again, of admitting 50,000,000 suspects into the puzzle. Or say a few thousand, if commonsense limited the thing to locals, counting Milchester as local.

Yes, it was objectively possible that Mrs Winfrey had seen some mate of Dorothy Sawyer's, previously unknown to her but sufficiently distinctive for Aidan Winfrey to have spotted him and made contact with him and blackmailed him. It was possible, but it was a rotten, untidy, inartistic answer.

Well then, the other person in the flat was not Dorothy Sawyer's accomplice but her rival: how did that fit? Somebody besides Mrs Addison, who also came for the money, and got some of the money, and was seen taking it, and so had to give some of it to the Winfreys? Somebody Rose Winfrey recognized, but who was not necessarily known to Dorothy Sawyer at all? Somebody who either had a key to the flat, or who used the door after Dorothy Sawyer had unlocked it?

Jim Gundry, come back to keep an eye on things, and giving way to temptation? No, no. That would be like a greenfinch making a swallow's mud nest in a barn.

Who, then?

In one sense it didn't matter, since he and Natasha were now clear and clean and readmitted to society, much though the village regretted and resented this. But they were right, those women who were ganging up on him. His pride was involved. He had been wrong about one thing, but he was right about this other thing, and he would prove it.

The thought of proving it filled him with despair and fatigue.

Natasha could now go back to her cousin's cottage in the village; she did so, for clothes and baths. But she slept at the Malletts', and spent most of her time there. Her excuse was sometimes that old Mrs Mallett needed her, sometimes that she there had the quiet and solitude she needed for preparing herself for her audition. There was a grain of truth in both excuses.

Dan overheard Natasha, for the hundredth time, telling his mother about her family. For old Mrs Mallett, as Dan knew, it was a joy and a sort of torture. It was the family of a dream. One of Natasha's brothers was following his father into accountancy; the other had a junior but promising managerial position in one of the giant oil companies; her sister was personal assistant to a man (a perfect gentleman, by all accounts) who ran something called a management consultancy. Natasha herself was the only Bohemian, and she was not very Bohemian. She had not rebelled against her family nor been disowned by them. She had not betrayed them, as Dan had betrayed his mother.

At three in the morning, in front of the kitchen range, Natasha gave Dan a somewhat different picture of her sister from that which she had projected to his mother. The sister was a po-faced conformist prig, and considered Natasha a wild pickle, liable to bring her parents' grey hairs in sorrow to the grave. But Natasha said that, deep down, Natasha and Pam (Nancy and Pam) adored one another, and always would.

'She's never told a lie in her life, but she'd tell any whopper to get me out of trouble,' said Natasha.

'Like me and my old lady,' said Dan. 'She disapproves of me just as much as – as Jim Gundry does. But she'd do bloody murder to keep me out of jail.'

'I think Pam would murder for me,' said Natasha. 'I think I'd murder for her. Even though, at home, we're always clawing at each other, and getting on each other's nerves, and stumping out of rooms in a rage, and being rude about each other's friends . . .'

'Being rude about each other's children,' said Dan abstractedly, bothered by an elusive memory.

'We haven't got any children, idiot.'

'Other sisters have. Oh my God. I've just got it.'

'I've heard that before.'

'Yes. I was wrong, but I wasn't as wrong as I thought I was.'

Sleepily, Natasha forbade further conversation about the murders. Dan, she said, was still trying to prove himself not quite such a fool as he had made himself look, and he was wasting time and breath, both of which were required for other purposes.

Dan had got it, but he had lost confidence in himself. He had had a clear, an utterly convincing picture of the grisly midnight events in Lady Dodds-Freeman's flat once before: a picture with the force of revelation: a moral certainty. Now he had a new moral certainty, and with it an army of doubts. It was not primarily a question now of convincing other people that he knew how and why Aidan Winfrey had been killed: it was a question of convincing himself.

There could be no more guinea-pigs, no more tethered goats. This was not because the risk to the bait was unacceptable, but because the risk of another humiliation to himself was unacceptable.

At four, and five, and six in the morning, lying intermittently wakeful in Natasha's arms, Dan pondered ways of proving, at last, and to himself, that he was right.

Mrs Addison was finally buried, since the police inquiries were complete and a suspect, who had made a full confession, had been remanded in custody. Mrs Addison's two daughters did not fly all the way home for the funeral, from the remote places where their husbands worked. This caused surprise and disapproval in the village. It did not seem to surprise Mrs Heron. It did not surprise young Mr Guy Heron, who remarked in the Chestnut Horse that fifteen hundred quids' worth of return air fare was too much to ask anybody to spend on a funeral.

Having a sister was outside Dan's experience. Having anybody intimately close to him, over a long period, was outside his experience. He had been, with qualifications, close to his mother all his life, but that was evidently quite a different thing. He had been close to a number of girls, but never for a very long time, and that was also quite a different thing.

On the subject of sisterly relationships he needed more detail, more colour. Natasha was puzzled by his questions, but she answered them as honestly as she could. She thought it was simple curiosity on a topic which, by the accident of birth, she knew more about than he did.

Dan's questions became macabre, and Natasha was uneasy answering them. Yes, she said reluctantly, if Pam were driving herself, were drunk, and killed herself, but killed or harmed nobody except herself, Natasha would lie to protect her memory. She would do so for their parents' sake, for the family's sake, for her own sake, and for Pam's sake. Pam, she thought, would lie to protect Natasha's memory, if the circumstances were reversed.

Would she do more than lie – commit shocking violence – to protect the reputation of somebody already dead? Yes, perhaps, because of the feelings of other people.

Dan believed Natasha; not only was she being as honest as she knew how, but also she was telling him things he wanted to hear. Every word confirmed his new revelation of the facts of Aidan Winfrey's murder.

He wondered if, now that he knew (kind of knew), he really wanted to do anything about it. He felt sorrier for the victim of blackmail than for a dead blackmailer. But there had been something extra dreadful about that chestless corpse in the rain.

And he wanted to retrieve his self-esteem.

Aidan Winfrey remained unburied. Evidently police inquiries were continuing, though it was given out that the file was closed. Dan was sure that the funny, twisted minds of the police were moving as his own mind had moved; he was also sure that they had not been vouchsafed his revelation because they did not have the benefit of Natasha's sleepy, whispered conversation in the small hours of the morning.

The day came for Natasha to go to her audition, in a theatre in a big city in the Midlands. Old Mrs Mallett redoubled her efforts to prevent this hitch to her plans. She had shooting-pains; she contrived a kind of fall; she simulated tears; she acted with brio and commitment, like someone in an old-fashioned film farce. Dan watched the whole performance with amazement. It was like nothing that had ever happened before, and he was no nearer understanding it.

In spite of the histrionic hours, Natasha went off in Guy Heron's car to catch the London train from Milchester station.

She said she would be back. Since she took only an overnight bag, it seemed that she meant it.

Dan had given Natasha questions to ask Guy Heron. They could be asked and answered in the time it took them to drive to the station. Natasha did not understand the point of the questions, but she promised to ask them anyway.

She telephoned her cousin in the village at 7.30, by arrangement, having arrived at her destination. Dan was there, being given a glass of sweet sherry by Natasha's cousin Edith Young. Edith Young chirruped about Natasha's journey, then handed the telephone to Dan.

'Mrs Addison's daughters,' said Natasha, 'Yes, well. Guy doesn't know them very well, though they're first cousins, because they're a bit older, and they've both lived mostly abroad since they married. What Guy does is envy them bitterly, but at the same time he despises their husbands.'

'Envies them why?'

'Money and success and position and stuff.'

'Despises their husbands why?'

'Square and dull and old.'

'Two sides of the same coin . . . What do the husbands do?'

'One's Far Eastern director of a shipping line. The other's a specialist in tropical diseases. And their wives, Guy Heron's cousins, are both apparently the local queens of wherever they are.'

'Ah. No breath of scandal attaches. Nothing nasty anywhere. Caesar's wife. Two wives of two Caesars.'

'Is that what you wanted to know?'

'Clarified my mind something beautiful. Thank you, love. Did Guy say anything about his mother's attitude to these nieces of hers?'

'Yes. In private she resents them being so rich and grand, but in public she never stops boasting about them. D'you remember Mrs Elton in *Emma*?'

'Yes and no,' said Dan.

'Always banging on about her sister. Like that, Guy says.'

'Ah. Every moment everything becomes clearer, except the things that don't. Good luck tomorrow.'

After an exchange of endearments muted by Edith Young's presence, Dan hung up. He finished his sweet sherry with difficulty, thanked Mrs Young, and bicycled home pondering.

As so often in the previous weeks, there was one supremely obvious and right thing to do, which suffered from the single disadvantage that it was impossible. He got off his bicycle and sat on a bank: thought would be more difficult when he got home.

There was, of course, a lever with which Rose Winfrey could be moved. But Dan could not expose, or threaten to expose, her fraudulent invalidism without making admissions he was not keen to make – not only as to the use of a key to her back door in the middle of the night, but even knowledge of the whereabouts of a key to her door. Everybody at the moment thought he was a fool but not, in this particular imbroglio, a criminal. It would be nice to stop being known as a fool without, thereby, becoming known once again as a criminal.

It had seemed possible that, with her husband dead, Rose Winfrey would stop pretending. But she had not stopped. She still lived on a sofa, and people came and looked after her. Either she fooled the doctor, or he went along with it. This was odd – Doctor Smith in the village was neither gullible nor venal: he was one of the few people in the world for whom Dan felt almost unqualified respect. (The respect had something to do with Doctor Smith's skill with a fly-rod.) But in the matter of Mrs Winfrey, the doctor *was* either a gull or an accessory. That was not the least odd part of the whole odd picture. Dan wondered if Rose Winfrey had anything on Doctor Smith.

The thing was to trick, persuade, cajole, lure or force Rose Winfrey into making a clear demonstration, to Dan and no other, of her physical fitness. And that was the impossible bit. Dan had fleeting mental pictures of pieces of meat being drawn on strings away from the lairs of furtive but predatory animals. Mrs Winfrey was furtive and predatory, but what piece of meat did Dan have? What string?

Dan pondered meat and string. He considered using Guy

Heron as bait – Guy Heron kidnapped, threatened with hideous disfigurement – to bring Rose Winfrey out into the open. Any such operation would be crude, dangerous and unpredictable; it would expose himself, if it failed, to humiliation, and if it succeeded to all sorts of criminal charges.

Meat? String? Mrs Winfrey had money, comfort, security, a smoothly organized life, an ongoing if puzzling confidence-trick which deluded most of the world. She was impregnable.

Dan remounted his bicycle. Riding very slowly home, he saw old Dusty Chinnock with his beehives. Dusty had moved a few hives into a big field of oilseed rape belonging to Willie Martin, a sea of tall brilliant yellow now in midsummer, a source of food for the bees almost as useful as the linden trees. Dan's mother had once kept bees, until the family had all got bored with being stung. But that was before there was so much rape seeding itself on all the verges and headlands.

Dan stopped and put a foot down. Old Dusty was using his puffer to expel bees from a frame he had lifted from the hive. The puffer was simply a one-handed bellows, loaded with smouldering brown paper. The bees couldn't stand the smoke, although it did them no harm . . .

Dan had it.

Rose Winfrey was not to be pulled. She was to be pushed. Like a bee, she was to be pushed out into the open with a puffer, there to confess her fraud, and so be compelled to tell the truth about the murder she had seen, and so name the person who had murdered her husband.

Dan collected his materials and bided his time.

He missed Natasha very much. He thought an audition would only last a day, perhaps only a minute, but this one seemed to take a week. Probably that was good news, if Natasha getting a job so far away could be called good.

The day came: all elements in correct conjunction at the Monk's House. Rose Winfrey in, as always; old Lady Dodds-Freeman in but irrelevant, as long as Dan waited until mid-afternoon; Guy Heron away; Mrs Heron away, spending a day in London; no slaves, gardeners, daily women, electricians or plumbers; no deliveries due from grocers, butchers or wine merchants.

Dan had a little compunction about what he was doing, but only a little, because it was impossible to feel sympathy for Mrs Winfrey.

Inconspicuous as a sparrow, Dan got his key to Rose Winfrey's back door, and let himself in. He made a fire in the back passage, placing it so that she would have a clear run down the stairs and out of the front door. He made the fire with the stuffing of an old sofa which had been left on the rubbish-dump behind the Priory. The stuffing burned vigorously, because Dan had soaked some of it with methylated spirit. It burned with a kind of furious smoulder, emitting dense, whitish clouds of pungent smoke. In a minute or two the flat would become uninhabitable.

Dan heard Rose Winfrey scream. He hardened his heart. She knocked over the telephone. It was too late to telephone. She shrieked for help at the window. There was nobody to hear her. She was in no real danger, and Dan was doing no real damage.

Dan put the rest of the doughy stuffing on to his fire. Choking, he ran out and round to the front of the house. Rose Winfrey saw him, and shrieked.

'Ye'd best come on out,' he called to her.

'I can't! I can't!'

'Ye'd best try.'

She wailed that she couldn't, that to save her life she couldn't run out of her own front door.

Dan tried the front door. It was unlocked. He took a deep breath, and ran upstairs through the acrid, billowing smoke. Rose Winfrey, in a dressing-gown, was sobbing hysterically. Dan thought for a moment that the sobs were an act, but he saw they were genuine. He took her hand and ran downstairs with her. She shrieked at the sight of the open front door. She recoiled from it, back into the smoke. She had run downstairs perfectly well, but she could not run out of the door. The smoke seemed to press at them like a fat white hand. They were both choking. They were still in no danger, because the front door was wide open a few feet away. Rose Winfrey fought at Dan, refusing to go outside. He dragged her. Still she fought. She collapsed on the doormat, half inside the house, hiding her face, obviously terrified, evidently mad.

Dan was completely puzzled.

He ran through the ground-floor passage of the flat, found and filled a bucket in a garage, and put his fire out. Rose Winfrey saw and shrieked at the open back door, through which a draught was already clearing the smoke. She suddenly scuttled upstairs, like a crab, on all fours, her face close to the stair-carpet. It was an extraordinary way for a grown woman to go upstairs. She was still sobbing. Dan followed her. This had not turned out at all as he had expected. Evidently he had discovered something, but he did not know what.

'Don't tell anybody,' said Rose Winfrey through her sobs.

'That you can run up and down stairs?'

'That I can't go out of doors.'

'Why can't you?'

'I can't tell you . . . Yes, I'll tell you. I've got a mental illness. It's quite common, it's called agoraphobia. Doctor Smith gives me tranquillizers, but still I can't go out of doors in the daylight.'

'At night you can?'

'I don't mind in the dark. I take all my exercise in the dark.'

'Gum,' said Dan. 'Why pretend to have one illness when you have another?'

'I'm ashamed of being mentally ill, but I'm not ashamed to be thought physically ill. Surely you can understand that? You get sympathy if you're an invalid. You get respect. You don't get sympathy if you're crazy.'

'Overstating it a mite.'

'People are suspicious. They don't trust you. They despise you.'

'I see their point,' said Dan. 'Why did you go to Lady Dodds-Freeman's flat, the night Mrs Addison was killed?'

'I didn't! I did *not*!'

'Police will reconstruct the scene. Sharron Syme will identify you.'

'Why should I tell you? Why should I tell you anything?'

'Depends how widely you want it known,' said Dan mildly, 'that you can't go out of doors in the daylight.'

Again he felt a certain compunction. It was harder to fight it down this time, because what he was doing was crueller. But it was necessary. He was very near to having the truth of his theory proved.

'You're trying to blackmail me,' said Mrs Winfrey.

'There's been a lot of it about. Why did you go to that flat?'

'I heard a noise.'

'No sleeping-pill?'

'No. I get them on prescription, but I don't often use them.'

'You heard a noise. What kind of noise?'

'Banging about. In the old bag's flat. I knew there was a lot of money, and I thought somebody was trying to steal it.'

'Why not ring the police?'

'I didn't want the police,' said Rose Winfrey, who now seemed resigned to answering Dan's questions, 'I wanted the money. My husband needed it. But I didn't get any of it, I didn't touch any of it. I didn't do anything wrong. They can't punish you for wanting things.'

'Why didn't you go down and get it a bit earlier?'

'I didn't have a key to that flat.'

'Ah. But when you heard the bangs, you realized somebody had got in and so the door was probably unlocked. So you ran downstairs in your dressing-gown –'

'This one I've got on now. Are you sure that fire's out?'

'Yes. Smells a bit still, doesn't it? But it's out. What did you see when you got to the old lady's window?'

'That cleaning-woman killing Gwyneth Addison.'

'How? Was there a light on?'

'In the room beyond, the bedroom. There was light coming through the door. Not much, but enough to see by.'

'There was nobody else there?'

'I suppose the old bag was comatose in the bedroom. I didn't see her. There was nobody else.'

'But you saw something else?'

'I saw that Gwyneth Addison was also trying to steal the money. She'd picked up nearly all of it. She must have got there before the Sawyer woman came.'

'How do you know she was trying to steal it? Perhaps she was just collecting it up, out of kindness, same as I tried to do earlier?'

'No, she was holding armfuls of it. The Sawyer woman was trying to grab it away from her. Gwyneth Addison said, "I need it. I need it more than that old drunk does, and more than you do." The Sawyer woman used a rude word and hit her with a bottle. If I'd tried to get any of the money, she would have hit me with a bottle too. She's much bigger than I am.'

'So then you blackmailed Mrs Addison's sister, using your husband as agent. Mrs Heron paid up a bit, to protect her dead sister's memory, and especially, I suppose, to protect those nieces she was so proud of. But he turned the screw too hard, because he had a greedy girlfriend who'd seen you looking in at the window. But Mrs Heron didn't have much money and she couldn't go on paying. So she shot him with her son's gun.'

'Yes, I know.'

'Didn't you care?'

'We hadn't been properly living together for years. He was always chasing little sluts. He cost me too much money. It was his own fault at the end that he made a mess of it.'

'The police must have interviewed you?'

'Yes, of course. I told them I was asleep. I said I might have left the light on, but I'd taken a pill and I was asleep.'

'Why didn't you tell them what you saw?'

'How could I? How could I tell people my own husband was a blackmailer?'

'Or, putting it another way, that you were?'

'I couldn't tell them anything. They'd make me give evidence in a court. I couldn't go into a witness box, out there in a courtroom. How *could* I? You're blackmailing me into telling you all this. Your beastly smoke – you're as bad as I am. You're blackmailing me because you know I'm mentally ill.'

'Seems to me you manage pretty well,' said Dan.

He had some sympathy with Mrs Winfrey, because he had seen her abject inability to go out into the open air by daylight, her real misery and helplessness. But his sympathy was heavily qualified. She had blackmailed, effectively killed her husband thereby, and within days she had been in bed with a lusty young lover.

'You'll have to tell the police what you've told me,' Dan said to her. 'I'll tell them you're going to. I'll use your telephone, if you don't mind.'

He rang the station in Milchester. She made no effort to stop him.

He left her sitting huddled on the sofa in her dressing-gown, a pretty horrible but also pitiable person wondering what was going to happen to her.

'Agoraphobia,' said the Detective Chief Superintendent. 'Of course everybody's heard of it, but I've never personally met a case before. Obviously it leads to a strange way of life. I never guessed. When we interviewed her, it was in her own flat, naturally, where she was all right. There was no reason to guess she couldn't go out of doors. After what you told us, and after what she told us the second time we saw her, we had to take her into Milchester to make a statement. It was a business getting her to the car. We had to have a nurse to help, and in the car she had to sit on the floor with a rug over her head. That is, according to the doctors, normal for victims of that disorder. She says she told her husband what she had seen on the night of the murder, as any wife would. She says she didn't tell us, because of her fear of having to go into the witness box in the wide open spaces of a court. She accepts that, probably, her husband then blackmailed Mrs Heron. She says she knew nothing about that, and never saw any of the money.'

'Are ye in way o' believen un?' asked Dan.

'Only her late husband could tell us how far she was in his confidence. Of course he was greedy, or they both were, so he got himself killed. I suspect she knew exactly what was going on, and that was the real reason for her withholding her evidence. I doubt if we can prove it. I doubt if charges will be brought. What I don't understand is how you got the idea that Mrs Heron would go to such lengths to protect the reputation of her dead sister.'

'A-ben larnen about sisters,' said Dan, twisting his cap in his hands. 'A-ben a scholard on subjeck o' sisters.'

'So it appears. Curious case. I have some sympathy for Mrs

Heron: blackmail is almost an uglier crime than murder. I think the jury will convict, but I don't think the judge will be severe. How did the fire start in Mrs Winfrey's flat?'

'Cigarette lef' a-smoulderen on a cushion?' suggested Dan.

'I suspect you of at least eight more or less serious crimes during the past month, to which we now add arson. Get out of my sight, and if you possibly can stay out of it.'

Dan nodded, gave his idiot grin, and trotted away to meet Natasha's train.

'They kept calling me back and calling me back,' said Natasha. 'And then there were only three of us left. And then they made me read the part they were considering me for. Audrey, in *As You Like It*. And I got it! Card and everything, and a job anyway until Christmas!'

'Great,' said Dan unhappily. 'What clinched it?'

'Well, she's a country wench, a kind of peasant, so it was all a question of the accent. I, hum, put on a, hum, old-fashioned sort of accent, imitating someone I'd heard . . .'

'Imitating who?'

'Your mother,' said Natasha.